ONLY YOU CAN PREVENT AN ALIEN INVASION

Congratulations, citizen.

If you are reading this, one of two things happened:

- We've averted the invasion and released this manual as a 'what-if' guide.
- The invasion has already begun.

This manual will not save you. But, it might buy you enough time to confuse the enemy, confuse your neighbors, or at least confuse yourself into believing you stand a chance.

Remember: survival is 10% preparation, 10% luck, and 80% not being noticed.

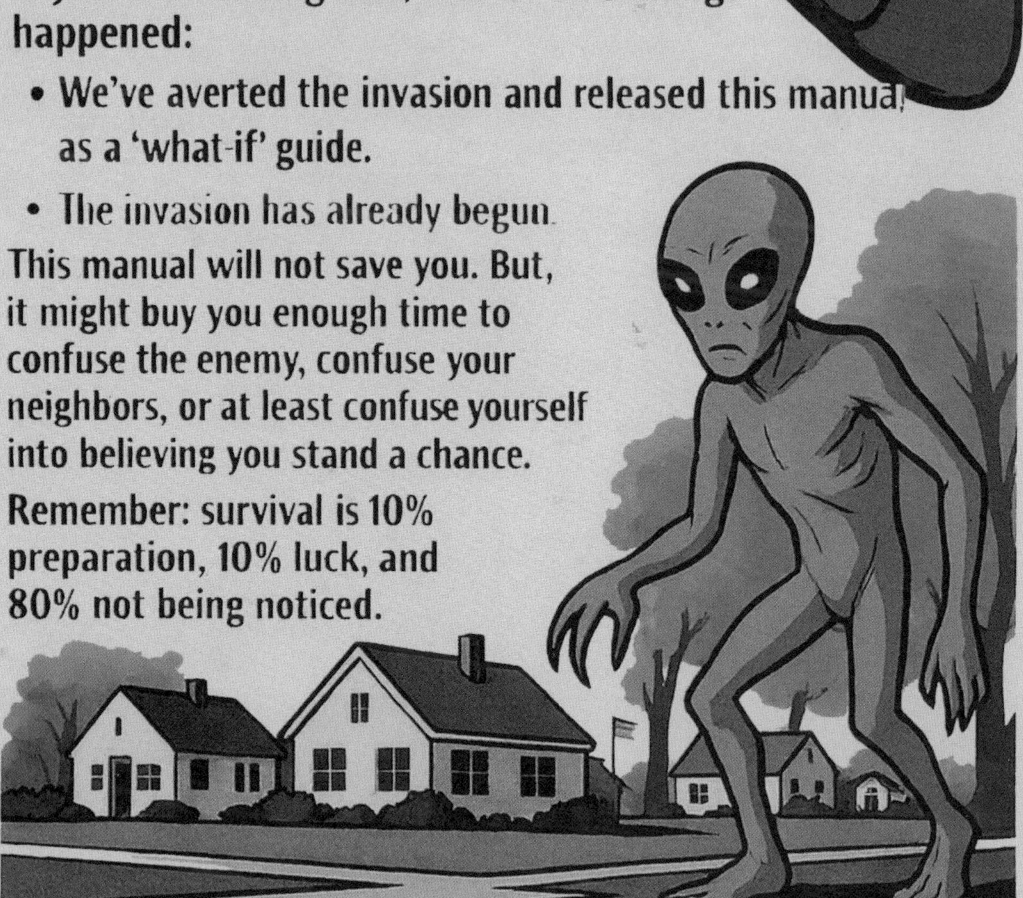

Dedicated to
SPC B.
Not AWOL.
Missing.
Some of us
still remember.

TABLE OF CONTENTS:

1. BASIC TYPES OF ALIENS
2. IMPROVISED DEFENSE
3. SIGNS YOUR NEIGHBOR HAS BEEN REPLACED OR JUST IMPLANTED
4. HOW TO DETECT AND REMOVE ALIEN IMPLANTS
5. DATING IN A WORLD UNDER SIEGE
6. WAYS TO HIDE
7. EDIBLE FOODS THAT YOU CAN SCAVENGE
8. ALIEN SHIPS AND THEIR ENGINES

CAUTION
KNOWLEDGE IS
DANGEROUS

==
⚠️ CIVIL DEFENSE MANUAL - 1959 EDITION ⚠️
==

PUBLIC NOTICE
OFFICIAL DISCLAIMER

This publication is an independent survival guide and is NOT AFFILIATED WITH or ENDORSED BY any branch of the United States Government, the Department of Defense, or the All-domain Anomaly Resolution Office (AARO).

For official information, reporting protocols, or to submit a credible sighting, the public is encouraged to use the AARO's authorized reporting portal:

👉 www.aaro.mil/reporting

This manual is presented FOR "INFORMATIONAL" AND "ENTERTAINMENT" PURPOSES ONLY.

The contents herein are based on unverified reports, historical rumors, and alleged "declassified" materials of uncertain origin. Readers are cautioned not to substitute this manual for an actual emergency.

By continuing to read, you acknowledge that:

- The publisher assumes NO LIABILITY for actions taken based on this document.
- The information contained within may be incomplete, inaccurate, or intentionally misleading.
- Any resemblance to actual classified procedures is purely coincidental... probably.

WARNING:

Possession of this pamphlet may draw unwanted attention from agencies both foreign and domestic.

PROCEED AT YOUR OWN RISK.

CHAPTER 1:
BASIC TYPES OF ALIENS

CLASSIFIED

RECORD INDEX
No. 1-295-A

FILE NO. 1

SUBJECT:

GREY ALIENS

CLASSIFIED

INDEX: 1A-001
REF: DOSSIER/ALIEN/GREY

DOSSIER

TOP-SECRET

GREY ALIENS

TOP-SECRET

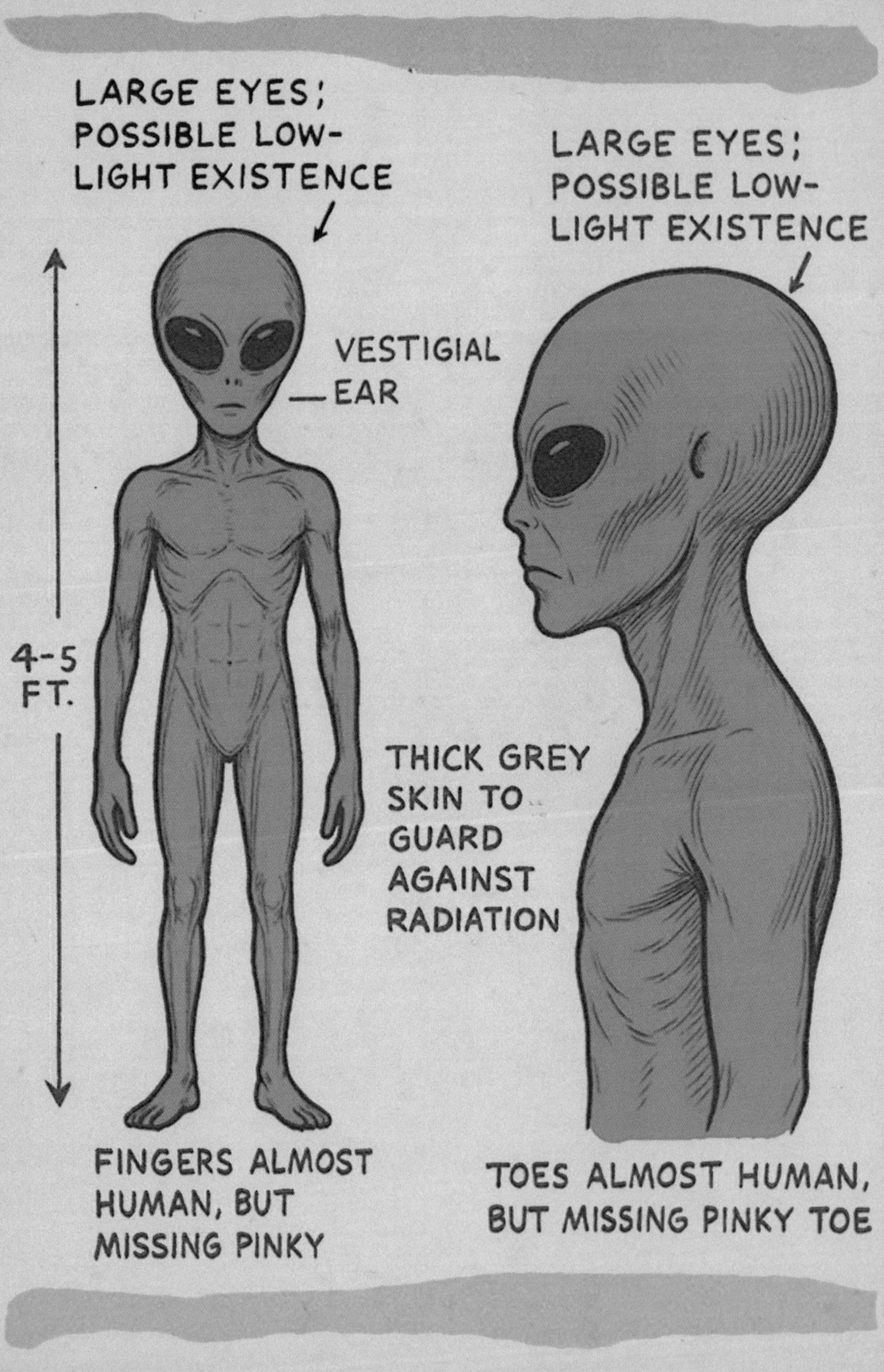
LARGE EYES; POSSIBLE LOW-LIGHT EXISTENCE
LARGE EYES; POSSIBLE LOW-LIGHT EXISTENCE
VESTIGIAL EAR
4-5 FT.
THICK GREY SKIN TO GUARD AGAINST RADIATION
FINGERS ALMOST HUMAN, BUT MISSING PINKY
TOES ALMOST HUMAN, BUT MISSING PINKY TOE

Codename: GREYS (Zeta Reticulans)
Origins: Survivors of a failed time experiment; possibly from Zeta Reticuli system (unconfirmed).
Estimated First Contact: Woking, Surrey; 1892 Possibly Earlier. Ships found in Iraq.
Physical Description: small, 3-4 ft. Grey skin, enlarged cranium, black almond-shaped eyes.
Behavioral Traits: Clinical, emotionless, efficient.
Known Objectives: Abduction, genetic experiments, possible hybridization with humans to make up for degraded DNA from space travel.
Threat Assessment: High-persistent abductions and secrecy.

CLASSIFIED

RECORD INDEX
No. 1-295-B

FILE NO. 2

SUBJECT:

HUMANOID ALIENS

CLASSIFIED

INDEX: 1A-002
REF: DOSSIER/ALIEN/HUMNOID

DOSSIER

HUMAN ALIENS

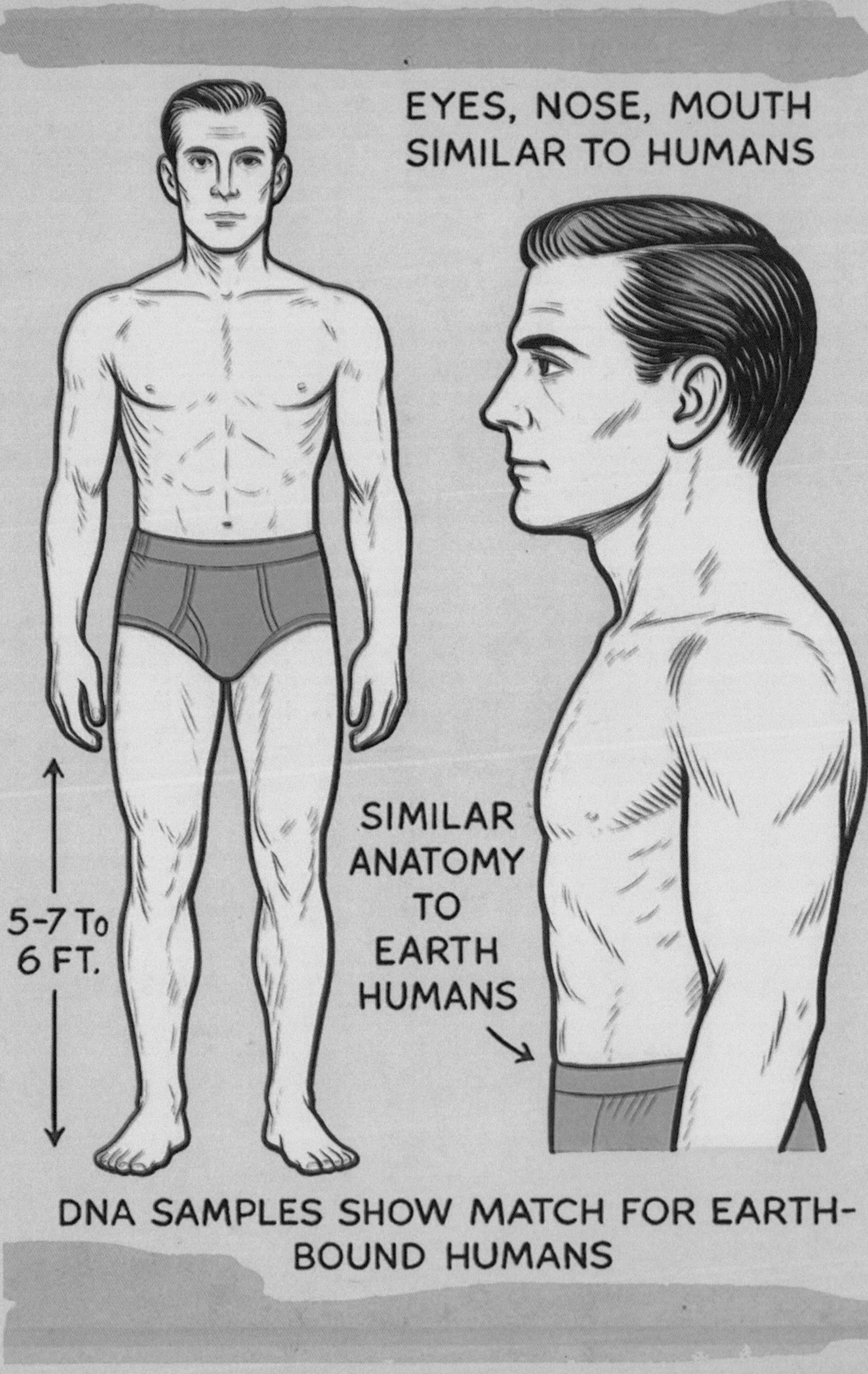
EYES, NOSE, MOUTH SIMILAR TO HUMANS
SIMILAR ANATOMY TO EARTH HUMANS
5-7 To 6 FT.
DNA SAMPLES SHOW MATCH FOR EARTH-BOUND HUMANS

Codename: HUMAN-TYPE (Manu-Kwehs, Nordics, etc)
Origins: Many worlds. Possibly seeded Earth, or vice versa. Possibly have common ancestors.
Estimated First Contact: Stories of human-types go back to pre-history. Stone-age petroglyphs.
Physical Description: DNA = Humans, with deviations. Some differences, maybe due to evolution trees.
Behavioral Traits: Same as Humans, maybe more stable.
Known Objectives: Unknown. Possible reunification. Anthropologically scientific in their research. Have been some difficult ones (i.e., Rance).
Threat Assessment: Similar to Humans—some threat.
Notes: Several species / Kardashev levels.

CLASSIFIED

RECORD INDEX
No. 1-295-C

FILE NO. 3

SUBJECT:

DRACONIAN ALIENS

CLASSIFIED

INDEX: 1A-003
REF: DOSSIER/ALIEN/DRACONIAN

DOSSIER

TOP-SECRET

DRACONIANS

TOP-SECRET

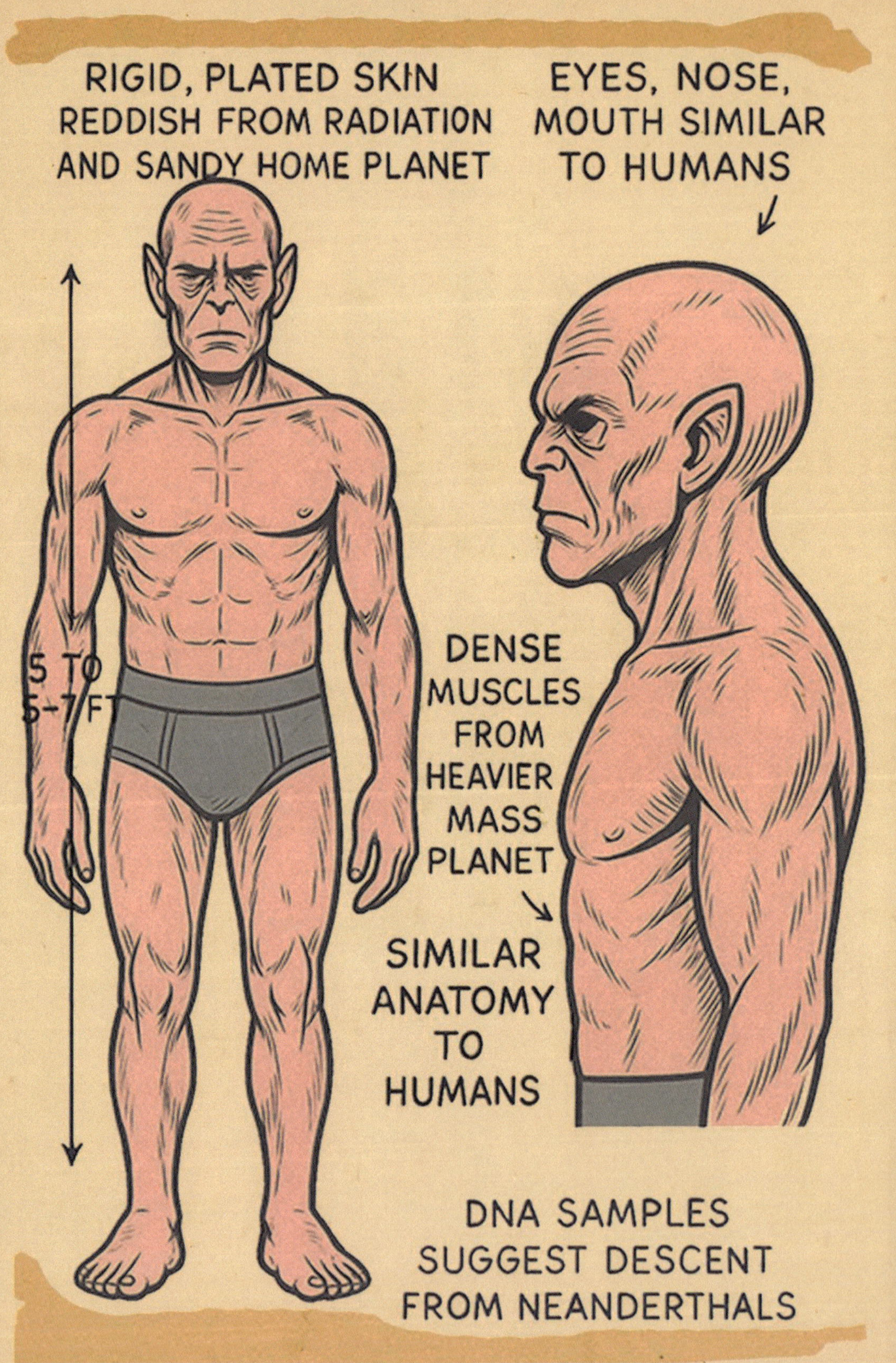
RIGID, PLATED SKIN
REDDISH FROM RADIATION
AND SANDY HOME PLANET
EYES, NOSE,
MOUTH SIMILAR
TO HUMANS
5 TO
5-7 FT
DENSE
MUSCLES
FROM
HEAVIER
MASS
PLANET
SIMILAR
ANATOMY
TO
HUMANS
DNA SAMPLES
SUGGEST DESCENT
FROM NEANDERTHALS

Codename: REPTILIANS (Draconians / Orion / Drax)
Origins: Unknown. Have stated they are looking for ancestral home.
Estimated First Contact: Rumors of contact on Earth, but only relics and bones found.
Physical Description: Humanoid reptilian. Dark eyes with nictitating lids, 5'-5'7" tall, muscular.
Behavioral Traits: Aggressive, territorial, militaristic.
Known Objectives: Planet conquest, genetic control, infiltration in humanoid societies, searching for an unknown lost "**homeworld.**"
Threat Assessment: **Hostile.**
Notes: Lost origins might be Earth.

CLASSIFIED

RECORD INDEX
No. 1-295-C

FILE NO. 3

SUBJECT:

MANTIDS

CLASSIFIED

INDEX: 1A-003
REF: DOSSIER/ALIEN/MANTIS

DOSSIER

TOP-SECRET

MANTIDS

TOP-SECRET

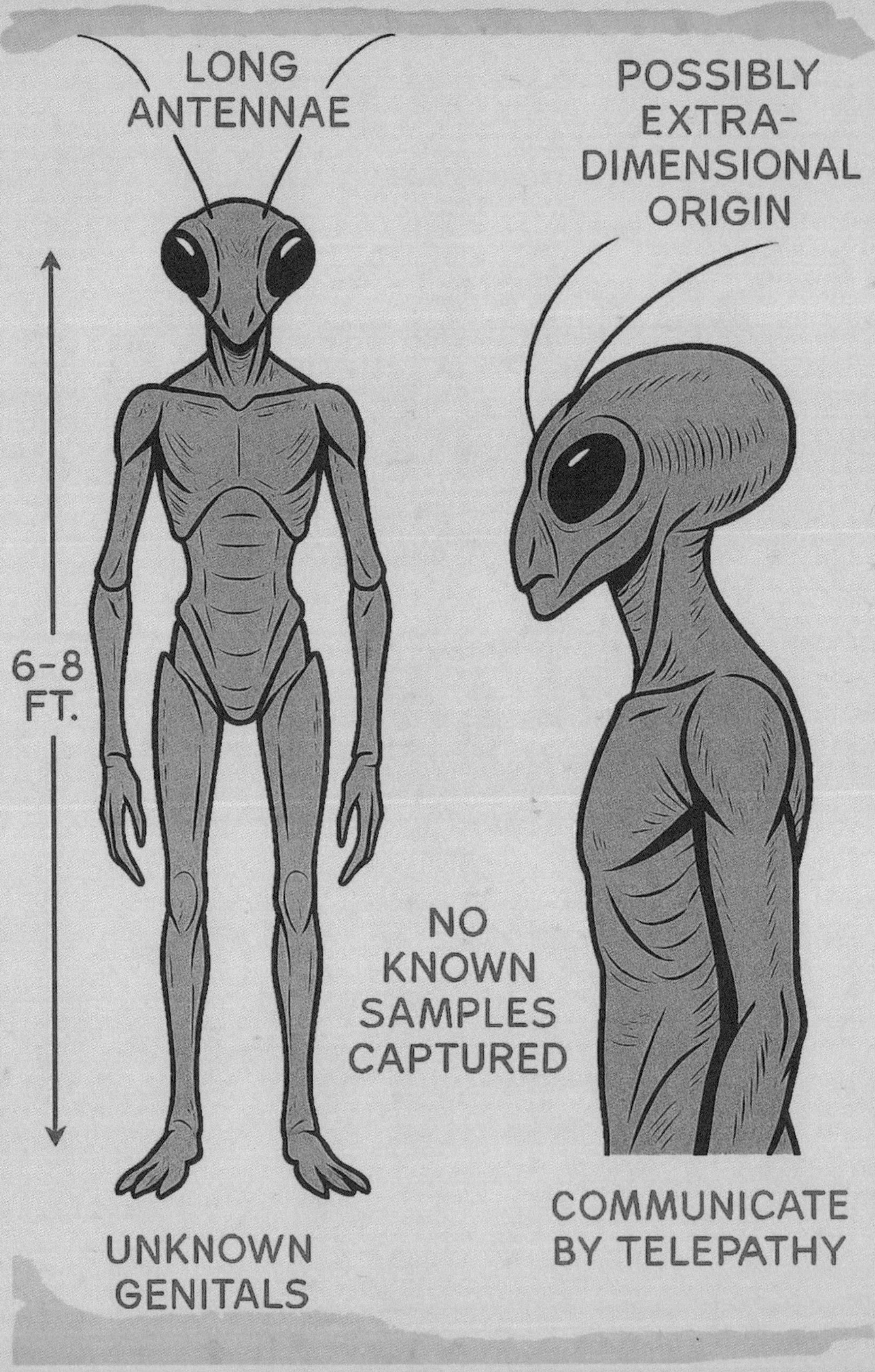
LONG ANTENNAE
POSSIBLY EXTRA-DIMENSIONAL ORIGIN
6–8 FT.
NO KNOWN SAMPLES CAPTURED
COMMUNICATE BY TELEPATHY
UNKNOWN GENITALS

WANDJINA ROCK FORMATIONS

Codename: MANTIDS (Ikaggen, Kachinas, Architects)
Origins: Unknown. Possible Extra-Dimensional. Can cloak or dimension-shift (unsure which).
Estimated First Contact: Stories of Mantids go back to pre-history. Stone-age petroglyphs.
Physical Description: No samples collected. Humanoid-Mantis-like in description.
Behavioral Traits: Telepaths. Detached. Calculating.
Known Objectives: Unknown. Possible long-term gene study or manipulation of humanity. Some reports say they act as custodians over other aliens.
Threat Assessment: Uncertain—motives unclear.
Notes: Their presence induces paralyzing fear.

CLASSIFIED

RECORD INDEX
No. 1-295-D

FILE NO. 4

SUBJECT:

SHADOW PEOPLE

CLASSIFIED

INDEX: 1A-004
REF: DOSSIER/ENTITY/SHADOW

DOSSIER

TOP-SECRET

SHADOW PEOPLE

TOP-SECRET

POSSIBLE ORIGIN OF:
VAMPIRES
LYCANTHROPES
BLACK-EYED CHILDREN

POSSIBLE ORIGIN: THE DARKNESS BETWEEN REALITIES

POSSESSES PEOPLE: CALLED **'DYBBUK'** IN JEWISH MYTHOLOGY

CALLED **'DJINN'** IN ARABIC MYTHOLOGY

CAN BE CONTROLLED BY ONE CALLED 'MASTER'

OR BY MR PERKINS

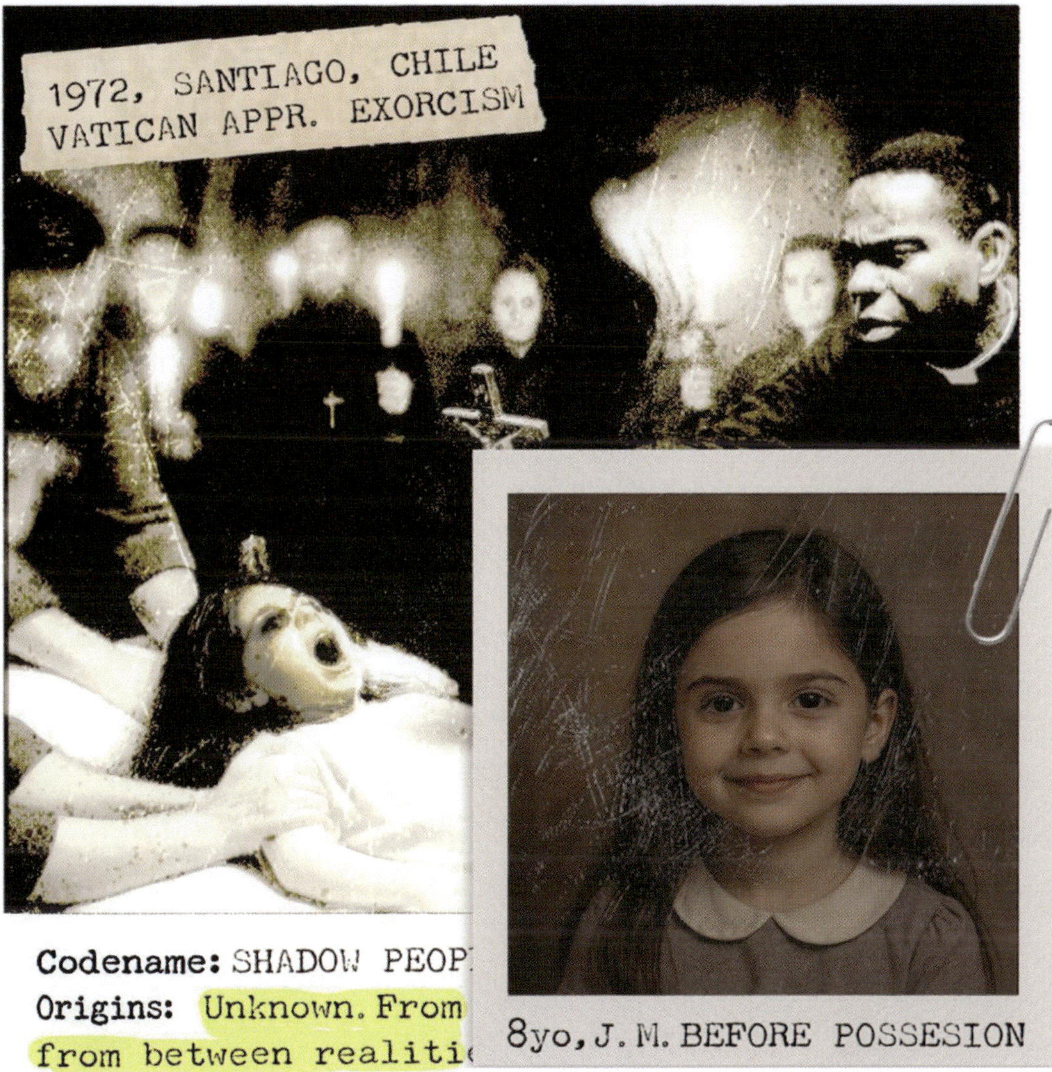

8yo, J.M. BEFORE POSSESION

Codename: SHADOW PEOP

Origins: Unknown. From
from between realiti

Estimated First Contact: Pre-Sumerian. Arrival prior to Younger Dryas event. Ask Mr. Perkins.

Physical Description: Dependant on human bodies they inhabit. Have limited physicalities without host.

Behavioral Traits: Aggresive. **Crave human flesh/blood.**

Known Objectives: Trigger return of 'MASTER'. Take human hosts to complete objective. Open door back to **'the dark place'**.

Threat Assessment: VERY HOSTILE.

CLASSIFIED

RECORD INDEX
No. 1-295-R

ENLIST TODAY

JOIN THE ARMY TO FIGHT THE ALIEN MENACE

THE THREAT IS REAL.

Enemy saucers have been sighted in our skies. The files are full. Civil defense cannot stand alone Your country needs YOU to enlist and join the fight against extraterrestrial invaders.

★ **Basic Training**
– weapons, evasive tactics, survival

★ **Alien Countermeasures**
– identification, containment, and report

TRAINING & DUTY

- Recruits receive 8 weeks of Army training: marksmanship, radar operation, containment procedures.
- **Benefits** – steady pay, food rations, medical treatment.

REPORT TO YOUR LOCAL RECRUITING OFFICE TODAY

TOP-SECRET

ENLISTMENT
CODE: 7-A-51

CHAPTER 2: IMPROVISED DEFENSE

ZETA • IMPROVISED DEFENSE

QUICK ID

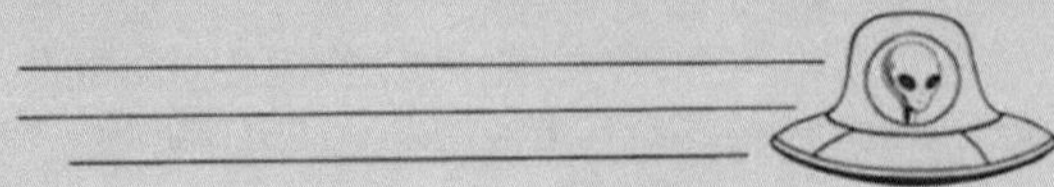

- **Abductors:** Tend to go for singles and pairs.
- Late-night suburb/rural encounters
- Small figures that look deceptively frail.
- Sensitive to bright light

CIVILIAN-LEVEL DEFENSE TIPS

- **Bright light:** Floodlights, bulbs, flashlights, laser pointers

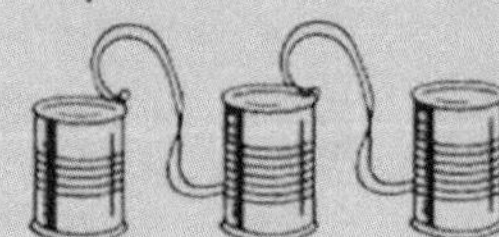

- **Mechanical Alarms:** Bells, cans, wadded aluminum foil, or broken glass
- **If you see the ship:** remain calm, call 911. Stay away. They tend to be radioactive.
- **Buddy-tether system:** When moving through woods at night, connect members via short rope or paracord loops so one person cannot be silently isolated. Two people are abducted faster than three.

- **Grounding Drills:** In case of paralysis or hallucinations, pinch self or control breath.
- **Watch the wildlife & vegetation:** Dead patches, silent birds, or animals avoiding a site can indicate alien activity –treat such spots as contaminated and leave.

ZETA • TACTICS & ENCOUNTERS

IDENTIFICATION IN THE FIELD

- **First sign:** Sudden radio static, even when equipment is powered off.
- **Environmental anomaly.** Eye witnesses claim an increase in static shocks.
- **Psychic Push:** Many report psychological effects. Some indicate hallucinogenic states. Telepathic words heard.

CIVILIAN SURVIVAL TIPS

- Stay in groups of three or more. Singles and Pairs have been known to be abducted.
- **Carry analog tools** (compasses work for alarm and direction; they react to alien tech by going haywire). Wear mechanical watches. Carry fire striker.

MILITARY ENGAGEMENT TIPS

* Do not engage. They have tech that can disable an entire nuclear base.

DO NOT engage if you are fatigued, nauseated, or disoriented. Zetas amplify human weakness.

HUMAN-TYPE
IMPROVISED DEFENSE

QUICK ID

- Most blend into Earth cultures. Hard to tell.
- Look for advanced tech, beyond normal.
- Some pose as scientists/politicians to fit in.
- Quite a few come as Anthropologists to study.

CIVILIAN-LEVEL DEFENSE TIPS

- Normal weapons work, unless they have healing implants. Then, EM pulse can halt healing.
- First known instance of EM pulse uncovering: Havana, Cuba. 2016 - Source Unknown.
- Other EM pulses uncovered implanted controlled humans, more than a few were politicians.
- Some instances of alien criminals have happened in the past. One instance, a criminal scientist came to Earth. He tried to use implants to control population.
- Said scientist had become a politician and blended in with governmentals. He ended up controlling a military facility in Utah.

- After he vanished, other embedded collaborators were found, but they also vanished after the Raid on Area 51 incident. September 2019.

HUMAN-TYPE

TACTICS & ENCOUNTERS

IDENTIFICATION IN THE FIELD

- **First sign:** UAP/UFO sightings. Possible crash. If land, they blend w/ people.
- **Environmental anomaly.** Unless they crash there will be none, except radiation.
- **Psychic Push:** Most have abilities like Humans, but some do have psychic abilities. Telepathy most prominent.

CIVILIAN SURVIVAL TIPS

- Do not approach. Most are scientific; can have criminal-type, like Humans.
- **Carry analog tools** (compasses work for alarm and direction; they react to alien tech by going haywire). Wear mechanical watches. Carry fire striker.

MILITARY ENGAGEMENT TIPS

* Do not engage. Some have implant tech that control Humans (i.e., Dugway).

DO NOT engage
Keep alert. Keep distance and watch. They will blend into Human crowds and vanish.

DRAX • IMPROVISED DEFENSE

QUICK ID

- Reddish to brown thick, scaly skin. Dark eyes.
- Height: 5ft to 5ft 7in. Hairless. Pointed ears.
- Hybrids- like short humans w/large brow ridge.
- Some rare hybrids look like pale, tall humans with blond or platinum hair and pointed ears.

CIVILIAN-LEVEL DEFENSE TIPS

- Their thick skin make normal weapons less effective. High-caliber reccomended.
- Their hybrids are more likely to seek colder climes, but Drax abhor cold, seek warmth.
- Caves are a good hiding place from Drax. Their sensors search for thermal signatures.
- The tall, pale hybrids are usually ostrasized, or killed at birth. They tend to be highly intelligent and have psychic abilities, and the Drax fear they would take over.
- Normal hybrids are close to humans in tolerance and are used for manual labor, livestock, and reproduction.
- Earth is not the only humanoid planet. Drax have hunted us before on their search for some long lost homeworld.

DRAX • TACTICS & ENCOUNTERS

IDENTIFICATION IN THE FIELD

- **First sign:** Watch for asteroids/meteors. They hide ships in large space rocks.
- **Environmental anomaly**. Any extra-solar comet/asteroid/meteor acting odd.
- **Psychic Push:** Drax have been rumored to have psychic ability to make them blend with background or people.

CIVILIAN SURVIVAL TIPS

- Shoot on site. They infest other planets, looking for resources and trying to find a lost 'HOME'.
- Their olfactory is more advanced. Stenches (ammonia, etc) make them recoil. Tear gas also. As does ice. They are from a desert planet.

MILITARY ENGAGEMENT TIPS

* Shoot on site. Most likely others are nearby. They negotiate as a trap.

⚠ Beware any impact craters! This could be a landing site. Drax are durable and plenty.

MANTIDS • IMPROVISED DEFENSE

QUICK ID

- Green or brown. Mantis-looking. Large eyes.
- Human-like forelimbs and triangular head with large compound eyes.
- Insectoid, upright posture; exoskeletal plates with glossy segmentation.

CIVILIAN-LEVEL DEFENSE TIPS

- Maintain open lines of sight - watch all approaches.
- Avoid travelling alone in dense brush/wooded areas or ruined structures.
- They are neutral and tend to be unsympathetic. They experimented on humans in past.
- Mantids do not attack, but will experiment. They use a psychic presence to stun subjects. Loud, irregular noise and heavy vibrations can distrub psychic abilities - use as a deterrent.
- If under their stun effect, concentrate on slow, steady breathing to break fear response and pinch self to break their hold.
- They work in companionship with the Zeta/Greys. They also share technology and some ships.

MANTIDS • TACTICS & ENCOUNTERS

IDENTIFICATION IN THE FIELD

- **First sign:** Many eyewitnesses feel fear. Many have also reported being frozen.
- **Environmental anomaly**. Time distortion. Silence of animals/insects. Pressure.
- **Psychic Push:** Witnesses describe telepathic messages, dreamlike commands, or sudden 'knowing'.

CIVILIAN SURVIVAL TIPS

- Do not run. Mantids move faster. They show cold, scientific interest in Humans. Try to appeal to that.
- Most eyewitnesses report them studying or manipulating, rather than killing.
- They may help against Drax.
- If frozen, concentrate on breath.
- If feel in danger, do not shoot.
- Conventional rounds are ineffective. High-Frequency weapons may work.

Mantids may be extra-dimensional
If encountered, try to reason
and learn more about their tech.

SHADES • IMPROVISED DEFENSE

QUICK ID

- Manifests: periphery, mirrors, or dark corners.
- Move through cracks, shadows, and reflective surfaces; tied to "between-realities" void.
- Appear as tall, featureless silhouettes – no facial detail.

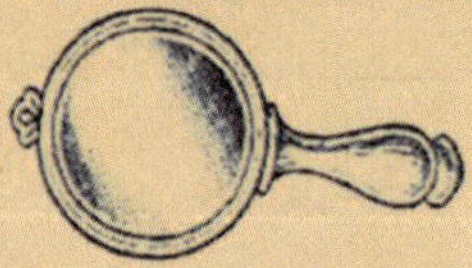

CIVILIAN-LEVEL DEFENSE TIPS

- Light as Defense: Flashlights, lamps, and flares repel. Sunlight and open flame destroy.
- Salt as Secondary Barrier: Lethal to them in direct contact; lay salt lines at doors and windows to block entry.
- Sacred Objects/Rituals: May weaken hold, but less effective than light, salt, or fire.
- Possession Signs: Sudden mood swings, aversion to light, burns in sunlight, and shadow-like movements.
- Response to Possession: Immediate exposure to light/fire or application of salt. Direct sunlight burns host if possession is active.
- Avoid Reflective Surfaces: Mirrors, still water act as portals. Cover during activity surges.

Stay Calm: They feed on fear. Slow breathing and emotional control reduce vulnerability.

SHADES • TACTICS & ENCOUNTERS

IDENTIFICATION IN THE FIELD

- **First sign:** An inexplicable feeling of dread or depression. They induce fear.
- **Environmental anomaly.** Heavy shadows. Cold spots. Animal absence in area.
- **Psychic Push:** Once they take possesion, they can take over the mind of kids. Older people may keep self-awareness.

CIVILIAN SURVIVAL TIPS

- They may take over friends/neighbors. Look for all-black eyes (even whites) May speak in growl voices.
- The children tend to yearn for flesh. Adults may feel the need to drink the blood of others (vampirism).
- They can only interact while in host.
- Children can be cleansed by exorcism.
- Adults may take more than exorcism, because shade can blend w/ self-aware host (mutual parasitic relationship).

They are afraid of direct sun! As per legends: they cannot be in sunlight. Bright lights weaken them. Silver kills.

DISCOVER HDDEN TREASURES
WITH A
GEIGER
COUNTER!
GEIGER
GEIGER
DETECT DANGEROUS
RADIATION!
• PINPOINTS WITH ACCURACY
• LIGHTWEIGHT, EASY TO USE!
FIND UFOs
GEIGER

CHAPTER 3:
SIGNS YOUR NEIGHBOR HAS BEEN REPLACED OR JUST IMPLANTED

SUBTLE BEHAVIORAL SHIFTS

1. Speech cadence off by a fraction.
2. Overly formal vocabulary.
3. Perfect recall of unimportant details, but forget shared emotional moments.
4. They no longer sneeze or cough, even during allergy season.
5. Blinking irregularities.
6. They hold eye contact just a second too long.
7. Avoidance of mirrors–or fascination with them.
8. Their gait changes.
9. Start using phrases lifted from local radio or TV verbatim.

10. **Overcompensating friendliness.**
11. Their pet avoids them—the dog barks, the cat hides, birds go silent.
12. Start waking at exactly the same time every night—you see the light flick on at 3:17 a.m.
13. No longer lock their doors.
14. They flinch at the sound of certain frequencies (phone vibrations, microwaves, doorbells).
15. Avoid old acquaintances—as if afraid to be recognized for what they're not.
16. Suddenly ambidextrous.
17. Unnatural stillness when resting.
18. They hum without realizing it —a low, almost subsonic tone.
19. They've stopped aging.
20. They heal too fast—or never seem to get hurt.

21. Faint hum or subsonic vibrations emanates from their house at night.
22. Curtains always drawn, but light leaks flicker rhythmically.
23. Plants near their property start dying or growing in stranger patterns.

24. Electronics glitch when they pass by—TV static, phones reset, Wi-Fi drops.
25. Mail addressed to someone else—yet they insist it's theirs.
26. Security cameras show static or distortions near their yard.
27. They leave garbage cans empty but always take them to the curb.
28. Delivery drivers refuse to go near their door.
29. Windows fog on the outside even in dry weather.
30. A smell like ozone, disinfectant, or formaldehyde wafts from vents.
31. Their car engine sounds off-pitch, like an electrical turbine.
32. Tools or wires visible through open blinds —copper coils, glowing panels, odd machinery.
33. Footsteps echo differently when they walk upstairs —too light or too synchronized.

34. No one ever sees them bring groceries home.
35. Every window replaced at once, but no contractors seen.
36. Package deliveries disappear from their porch instantly.
37. No reflections from their windows at night.
38. A faint smell of burnt plastic after they leave.
39. They mirror your gestures a beat too late.
40. Show no emotional reaction to local news or tragedy.
41. Forget your name, then overuse it once reminded.
42. Suddenly passionate about topics they never cared about—usually technical or cosmic.
43. Avoiding touch, claiming "skin sensitivity."
44. Use "we" instead of "I" unconsciously.
45. Display no startle reflex.
46. Refuse food from anyone else's kitchen.
47. Eyes reflect too much light, even in dim settings.
48. Neighbors disappear after visiting.
49. Government vans parked nearby whenever they're home.
50. They say, "Hi! I'm an alien."

SHELTER DOGS
CAN HELP DETECT ALIENS AND ANDROIDS IN THE COMING INVASION!
ADOPT ONE TODAY!

CHAPTER 4:
HOW TO DETECT AND REMOVE ALIEN IMPLANTS

WARNING: DO NOT ATTEMPT!

TO REMOVE YOUR OWN IMPLANT OR ANYONE ELSE'S, UNLESS YOU HAVE EXPERIENCE AND EXPERTISE IN THIS AREA

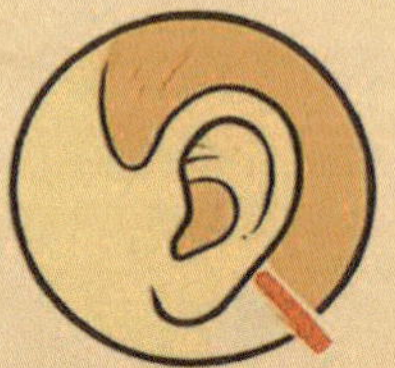

SUSPECTED IMPLANT ZONE

Alien implants are no laughing matter. Whether you suspect an abduction, a missing night's memory, or a mysterious lump behind the ear– ***don't extract it yourself*** !!!!

This technology operates far beyond human understanding. **Removal** without proper tools, sterile conditions, or medical expertise can cause:

- **Neurological shutdown**
- Hemorrhagic resonance (vibration-induced internal bleeding)

⚠ EVEN DURING AN INVASION OR EVACUATION, LOCATE A TRAINED MEDICAL PROFESSIONAL ⚠

-a doctor, field medic,
combat nurse,
or even a veterinarian
familiar with
livestock tagging tools.

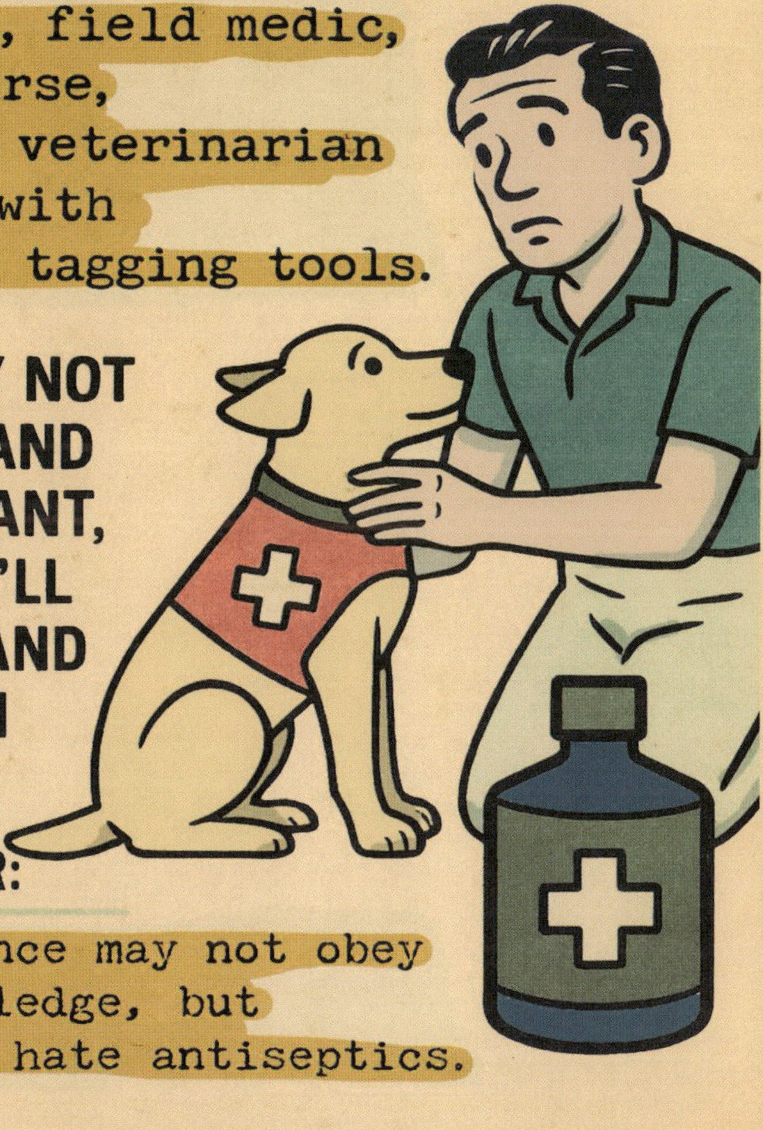

THEY MAY NOT UNDERSTAND THE IMPLANT, BUT THEY'LL UNDERSTAND INFECTION CONTROL.

REMEMBER:

Alien science may not obey human knowledge, but infections hate antiseptics.

HOW TO TELL IF YOU'RE A WALKING ANTENNA

Not all implants are visible. Some are microscopic, others phase between dimensions. Watch for the following common indicators:

- Persistent ringing in the ears (especially when UFOs are near.)
- Metallic taste in mouth during thunderstorms
- Dreams broadcast in "third person."
- Tiny geometric scars behind the ear, at the base of the skull, or between toes.
- "Missing time".

If you exhibit more than three of these symptoms, it's time for a **containment scan.**

You can use a handheld metal detector, a compass.

If the needle dances when you move your head, congratulations--you're a walking broadcast tower.

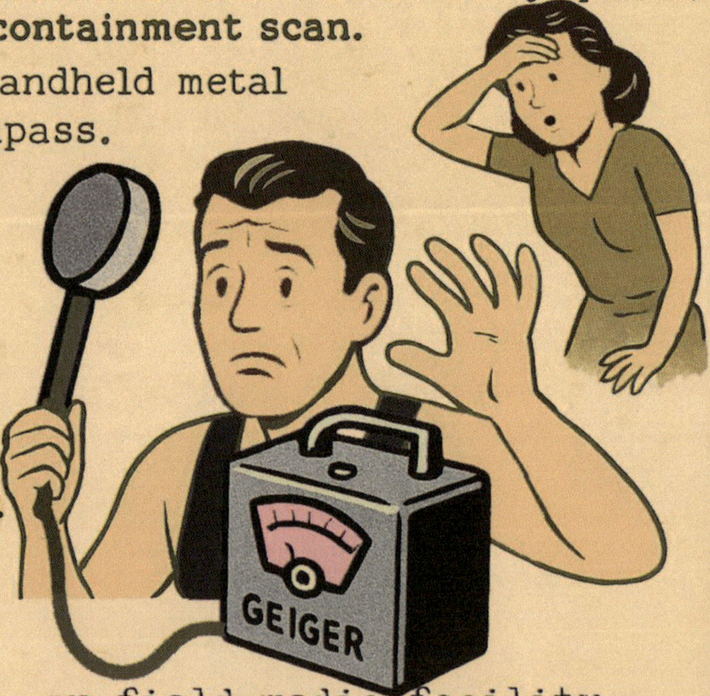

At any functioning hospital, mobile clinic, or field medic facility, ask for MRI or CAT scans. These can often reveal implants invisible to the naked eye.

WHAT TO DO AFTER EXTRACTION

- Store the implant in a lead container (a coffee tin wrapped in a copper wire mesh will do). Or use a microwave. They're lined with a Faraday cage to stop signals.

- Do not burn it. There's so much to learn.

- Contact the government UFO reporting office, or (in case of invasion) any field command.

Or in last ditch cases:

In the Dugway invasion, several **EMP** generators were used to disarm multiple implanted soldiers at once.

It's the same as what was used in the Havana Syndrome cases to free implanted ambassadors/politicians.

SHOW THEM
YOU LOVE
THEM
TACOS ARE
THE FOOD
LOVE
LANGUAGE
WITH
TACOS
ABUELA'S

CHAPTER 5:

DATING IN A WORLD UNDER SIEGE

HIGHLY
DISCOURAGED!!

This isn't a movie.

•Reproduction diverts attention from immediate survival. Emotional bonds and hormonal response can be used as weapons. Several aliens can track by pheromones, and loved ones can be used as lure

There'll be time after.

WHAT WORLD WOULD YOU BRING THEM INTO?
WAR'S UNKNOWN DURATION MAKES RAISING CHILDREN A CRUELTY.
UNTIL THE INVASION IS REPELLED, OR HUMANITY FINDS REFUGE, IT SENTENCES THEM TO SUFFERING.

- Alien-occupied zones may be contaminated or unsafe for childbirth, leading to high mortality rates.
- Governments or surviving factions could enforce population limits to maintain mobility, secrecy, and sustainability.
- Any colony or bunker system must carefully regulate population to sustain oxygen, energy, and food reserves.

ONLY YOU SURVIVE THE INVASION

INVEST IN THE PROMETHEUS SANCTUARY BUNKER TODAY

CITIZENS OF THE NEXT AGE—

- If you see this message, the time has come:
- The first wave is already in orbit

THIS IS NOT A SALES PITCH. IT IS YOUR LAST CHANCE.

At PROMETHEUS SANCTUARY, we built more than a bunker – we built a future.

WHY CHOOSE PROMETHEUS?

- 1.000 feet underground, shielded by electromagnetic deflectors
- Independent air/water/food systems rated for 10+–years
- Al-guided defense drones, perimeter force fields, stealth cloaking
- Luxury-dwellings, labs, vaults, gardens because survival doesn't have to mean struggling

ENROLLMENT OPENS NOW

Secure your spot. Sign your non disclosure.
One lifetime. One chance. One Prometheus.

YOUR ROLE. YOUR DUTY

You are not just buying a contract – you're electing to survive.

Only the prepared will have hope.

Only YOU can claim your place.

"Survival isn't luck – It's engineering, resolution, and secrecy."

PROMETHEUS SANCTUARY BUNKERS

WHERE BILLIONAIRES GUARD TOMORROW. (Ignore this at your own peri)

CHAPTER 6: PLACES TO HIDE

URBAN AREAS DURING AN INVASION

1. GROCERY STORES AND SUPERMARKETS

WHAT YOU'LL FIND:
Canned Foods, baby food, dry grains, rice, bottled water, first aid kits, batteries, lighters.

DANGERS:
Looters, collapsing shelves, rats, spoiled food, botulism from dented cans, tetanus.

TIPS:
Enter through loading docks.
Avoid walk-in refrigeration. They can block heat-sensors, but it's easy to become stuck.

2. SUBWAYS

WHAT YOU'LL FIND

Vending machines. Easy cross-town unseen movement. Possible subway/metro cars for housing.

DANGERS

Rodents and other disease carrying pests. Gangs. Other unhoused. Flooding. Cold winters. Limited movement. Aerosol/Gas weapons.

TIPS:

Hiding underground masks heat signatures from above. Watch for quakes and shaking due to alien weapons firing on buildings.

3. SCHOOL CAFETERIAS

WHAT YOU'LL FIND

Nonperishable foods, Utensils as weapons, School books to rebuild society (if they haven't been burned).

DANGERS:

Looters/Gangs, Food spoilage, Infected people, Emotional Trauma from childhood.

TIPS:

Schools make great make-shift shelters for a large group. Remember to board up the windows to not give away position. Also, use mylar blankets to mask heat-signatures from the outside.

4. GAS STATIONS

WHAT YOU'LL FIND

Canned foods, bagged snacks, bottled water, first aid kits, road medicines, batteries, lighters, tobacco.

DANGERS:

Looters, collapsing shelves, rats, spoiled food, botulism from dented cans, tetanus, flammable liquids.

TIPS:

Check abandoned cars for weapons or unused fuel. Hiding in the cars can limit heat signatures. Gas stations can also have microwaves to use as portable Faraday cages.

RURAL AREAS
1. FARMS

WHAT YOU'LL FIND

A place to grow vegetables, grains, and livestock. Farmers tend to have tools.

DANGERS

Farmers defending property, guard animals, hoarders, serial killers, unsafe structures

TIPS:

A lot of farms have storm shelters and/or root cellars that may contain preserves, in cans or jars. These can also mask heat signatures from alien or human sensors.

2. WOODED CAVES

WHAT YOU'LL FIND

Easier access to forest wildlife and scavenged foods. Easier to hide out invasions or government upheaval.

DANGERS

Moisture can lead to foot rot and can harbor cold climates that lower immune systems when fighting infections or colds.

TIPS

Caves hide heat signatures from aliens and humans. They can also be a source of fresh water, and the right ones can house many people in case of fall-out..

NEW! **From the Makers of CLEAN-BELLY LABS...**

CAMP-SAFE TABS

"Because Bad Beans Shouldn't Spoil the Fun!"

Uh oh! Did supper taste a little too ***wild*** last night? Don't let a case of the *Forest Fidgets* ruin your getaway!

- ✓ Calm your stomach faster than you can say *'burnt beans!"*
- ✓ Neutralize bad bacteria from mystery meats and dubious chili.
- ✓ Restore pep, smiles, and scout spirit!

Scientifically Tested! Doctor Approved!

Formulated by Clean-Belly Laboratories, the same fine folks who brought you ***GutGuard*** and ***Happy Tummy Tonic!***

Makers of: GutGuard *and* Happy Tummy Tonic!

PACK LIGHT, LIVE BRIGHT!

CHAPTER 7:
EDIBLE FOODS THAT YOU CAN SCAVENGE

REGIONAL FORAGING

NORTH AMERICA/EUROPE

Dandelion greens
(vitamin A, C)

Cattail roots & shoots
(vitamin A, B, C,
potassium, magnesium)

Pine nuts
(fat, protein, magnesium)

Green Onions
(vitamin C, fiber)

Caution: Open fires attract attention! Fresh food will be constant. Cans and Jars can spoil and spread disease.

REGIONAL FORAGING

NORTH AMERICA/EUROPE

Common Chickweed
(vitamin C)

Purslane
(vitamin C, Omega3)

Broadleaf Plantain
(vitamin A, C)

Kudzu
(vitamin A, C, K)

Caution: Always wash your vegetables before eating. Beware of poisonous look-alikes. Learn the differences.

EDIBLE MUSHROOMS

NORTH AMERICA / EUROPE

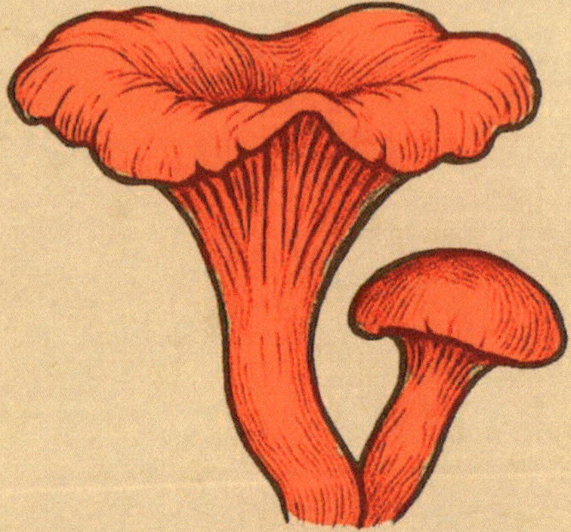

CHANTERELLE
(Cantharellus cibarius)

Vitamins / Minerals

PORCINI
(Boletus edulis)

Protein / Carbohydrates

OYSTER MUSHROOM
(Pleurotus ostratus)

Protein / Fiber

LION'S MANE
(Hericium eriaceus)

Protein

EDIBLE MUSHROOMS

NORTH AMERICA / EUROPE

CHICKEN-OF-THE-WOODS

(Lastiporus spp.)

Protein / Carbohydrates

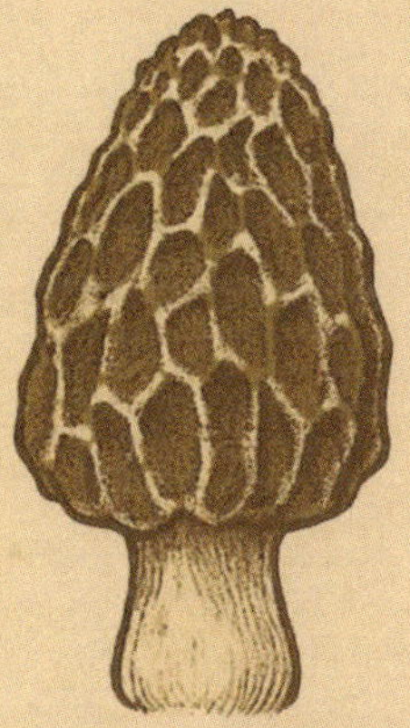

MOREL

(Morchella spp.)

Protein / Vitamins

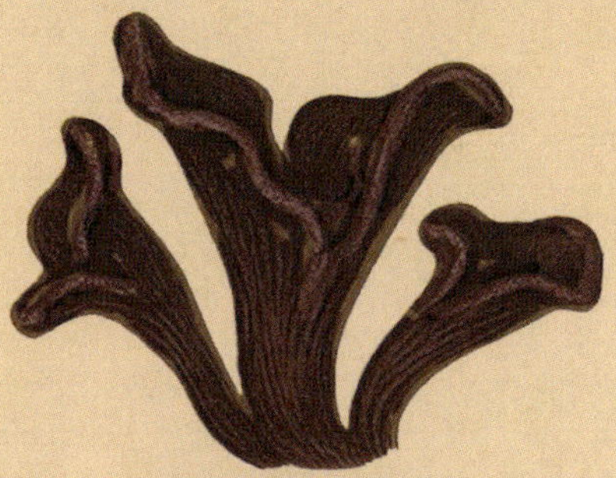

BLACK TRUMPETS

(Craterellus cornucopioiles)

Fiber / Carbohydrates

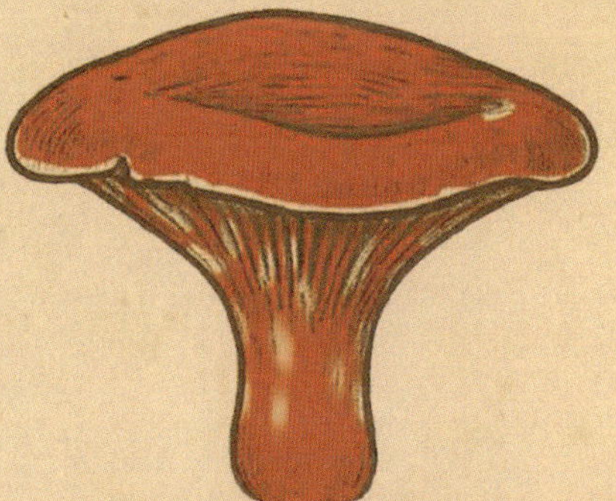

SAFFRON MILKY CAP

(Lactarius deliciosus)

Fiber

REGIONAL FORAGING

SUB-SAHARAN AFRICA

Drumstick Tree
(vitamins A, Bs, C, E, iron, calcium)

Baobab
(vitamin C)

Pumpkin leaves
(vitamins A, C, iron, calcium, protein)

Shea
(fat, vitamin C, calcium, potassium)

Caution: Eat only plants positively identified as edible. Cooking roots and tubers destroys toxic compounds.

REGIONAL FORAGING

SUB-SAHARAN AFRICA

Tamarind
(vitamins A,C)

Marula
(vitamins A,C)

Amaranth
(vitamin A, iron)

Jute Mallow
(vitamin A, C, iron)

Caution: For safe consumption of most questionable tubers and root vegetables, specific steps like peeling, soaking, and thorough cooking are often necessary, and if a tuber is very green or bitter, best to discard it.

EDIBLE MUSHROOMS
OF SUB-SAHARAN AFRICA

TERMITE MUSHROOMS
(Termitomyces)

Protein / C Vitamins

KING TUBER MUSHROOMS
(Pleuratus Tuber-Regium)

Fiber / Protein

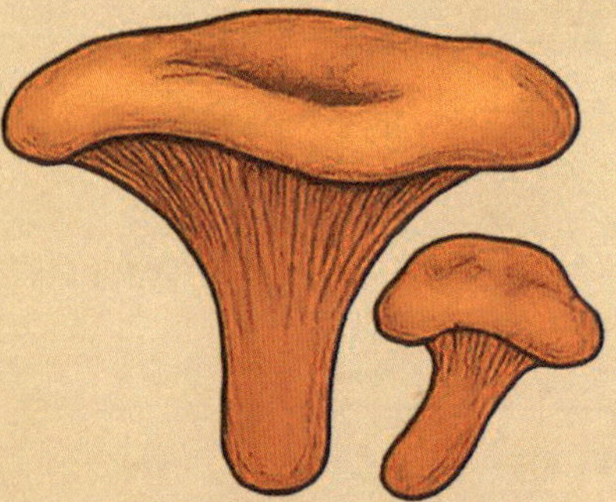

AFRICAN CHANTERELLE
(Cantharellus cibarius)

Vitamin D / Iron

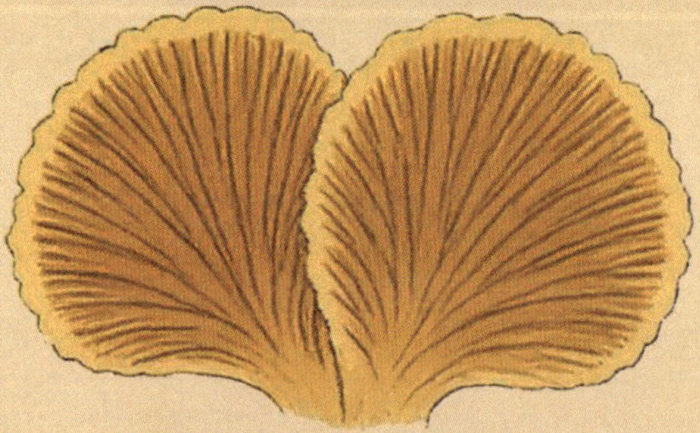

SPLIT GILL FUNGUS
(Schizophyllum Commune)

Fiber / Protein

EDIBLE MUSHROOMS
OF SUB-SAHARAN AFRICA

PSATHYRELLA TUBERCULATA
(Psathyrella tuberculata
Complex Carbs / Protein

STRAW MUSHROOMS
(Volvariela volvaceas)
Protein

WOOD EAR MUSHROOMS
(Aurricularia species)
Vitamins B / D

MILKCAPS MUSHROOMS
(Lactarius species)
Vitamin D / Protein

REGIONAL FORAGING

MIDDLE EAST

Dandelion
(vitamins A, C)

Wild Onion
(vitamin C, fiber)

Common Chickweed
(vitamin C)

Broadleaf Plantain
(vitamin A,C)

Caution: Avoid plants along channels or roadways.

REGIONAL FORAGING

MIDDLE EAST

Mallow
(vitamin C)

Wild Fennel
(vitamin C, potassium, calcium, and magnesium)

Date Palm
(natural sugars, C & B vitamins, and folate)

Fig
(vitamin K)

Cautions: Many desert plants store water in fibrous tissues that may cause stomach upset if eaten raw. Always boil or roast before eating.

EDIBLE MUSHROOMS
OF THE MIDDLE EAST

DESERT TRUFFLE
(Terfezia spp.)

Protein / Carbohydrates

OYSTER MUSHROOMS
(Pleurotus ostreatus)

Fiber / Protein

SHAGGY INK CAP
(Coprinus comatus)

Folate / Iron

PARASOL MUSHROOM
(Macrolepiota procera)

Vitamin D / Protein

EDIBLE MUSHROOMS
OF THE MIDDLE EAST

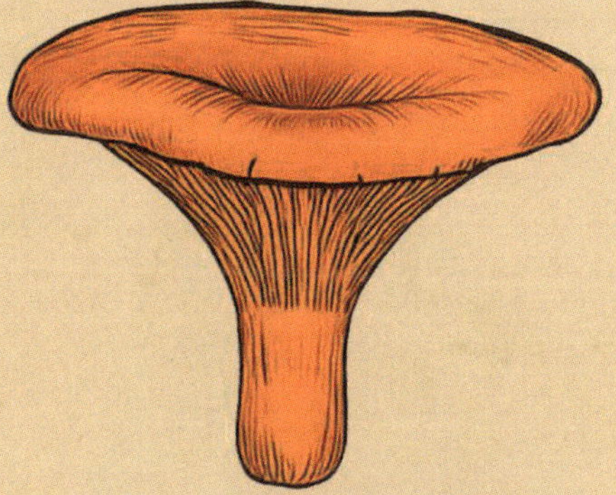

SAFFRON MILKY CAP

(Lactarius deliciosus)

Potassium/ Phosphorus/ Iron

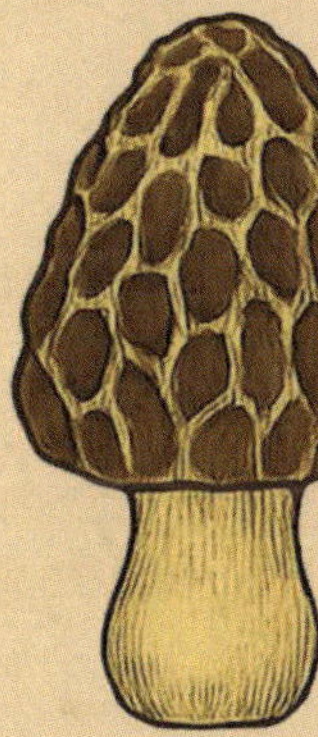

MOREL

(Morchella spp.)

Protein/iron/Vitamin D

KING BOLETE

(Boletus edulis)

Protein

JELLY EAR

(Auricurlaria spp.)

Vitamins B/ D

REGIONAL FORAGING

EAST ASIA

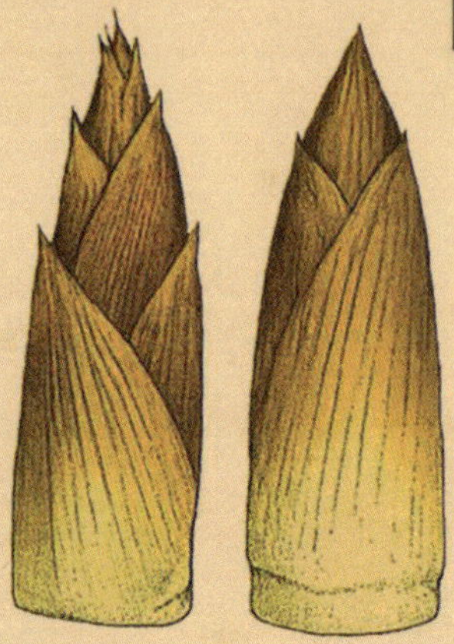

Bamboo Shoots
(carbs, potassium)

Japanese Knotweed
(vitamin C)

Fiddlehead Ferns
(antioxidants)

Burdock Root
(fiber, potassium)

Caution: Avoid foraging near rice paddies treated with pesticides.

Always cook ferns and shoots to avoid natural toxins.

REGIONAL FORAGING

EAST ASIA

Smilax Glabra
(Iron, Zinc)

Purslane
(Omega-3 Fatty Acids)

Lotus Root
(Vitamins C, B6, Calcium)

Mugwort
(Vitamins C, Bs, E)

Caution: Avoid harvesting in polluted areas or where agriculture is common.

EDIBLE MUSHROOMS OF EAST ASIA

SHIITAKE

(Lentinula edodes)

Vitamins B/D

MAITAKE

(Grifala frondosa)

(Hen of the Woods)

Vitamins B/D

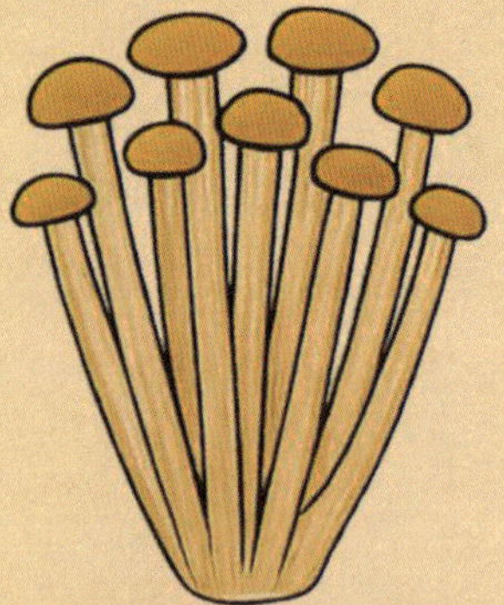

ENOKI

(Flammulina velutipes)

Vitamins B/D

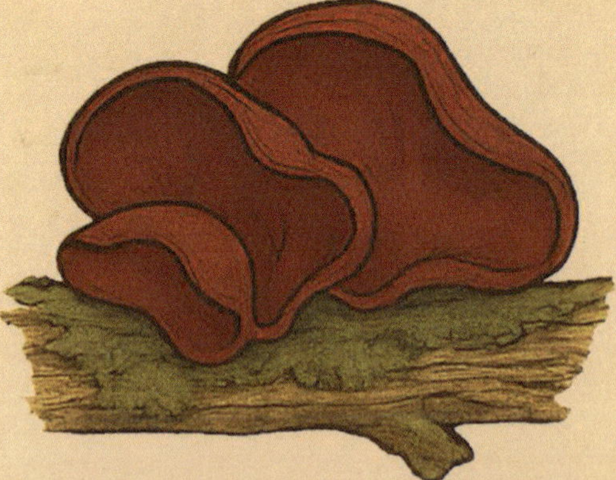

WOOD EAR

(Aurcicularia auricula-judae)

Vitamins B/D

EDIBLE MUSHROOMS OF EAST ASIA

MATSUTAKE

(*Tricholoma matsutake*)

Protein / Fiber

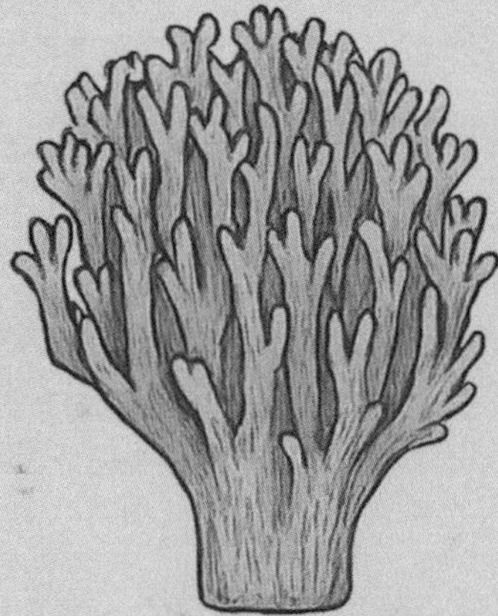

CORAL FUNGI

Fiber

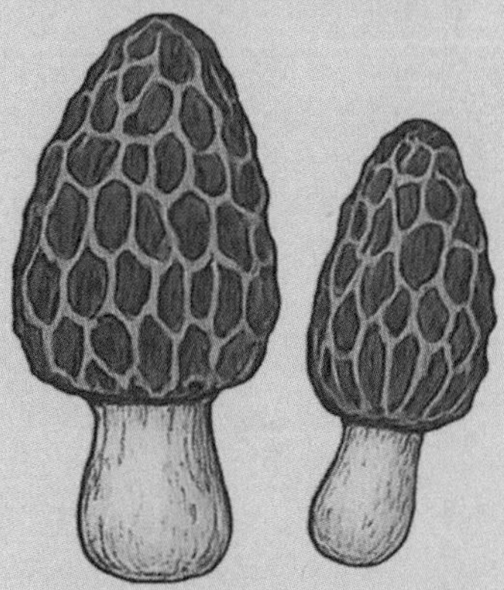

MORELS

(*Morchella spp.*)

Vitamins / Iron

LION'S MANE

(*Hericium erinaceus*)

Fiber

REGIONAL FORAGING

INDIA

Purslane
(vitamin C, Omega3)

Amaranth
(vitamin K, calcium, iron, magnesium)

Red Sorrel
(vitamins A, C, iron, magnesium, potassium)

Drumstick Tree
(vitamins A, Bs, C, E, iron, calcium)

Caution: Boil or cook all wild greens and roots to reduce toxins.

REGIONAL FORAGING

INDIA

Jackfruit

(Vitamin C, Potassium, Magnesium)

Indian Gooseberries

(Vitamin C, A, E, B6, B5)

Bael

(Vitamin C, Thiamine, Riboflavin)

Jamun Fruit

(Vitamin C, A, B-Complex)

Caution: Eat only plants positively identified as edible.

REGIONAL FORAGING INDIA

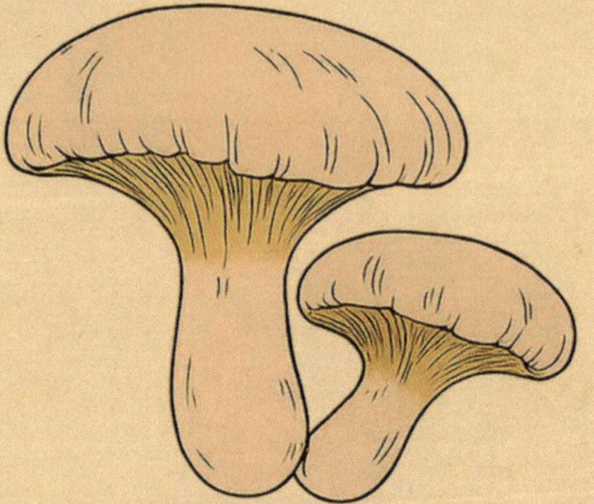

WHITE SHIITAKE

(*Lentinus squarossulus*)
Vitamins B / D

Russula

(*Russula senecis*)
Vitamins B / Protein

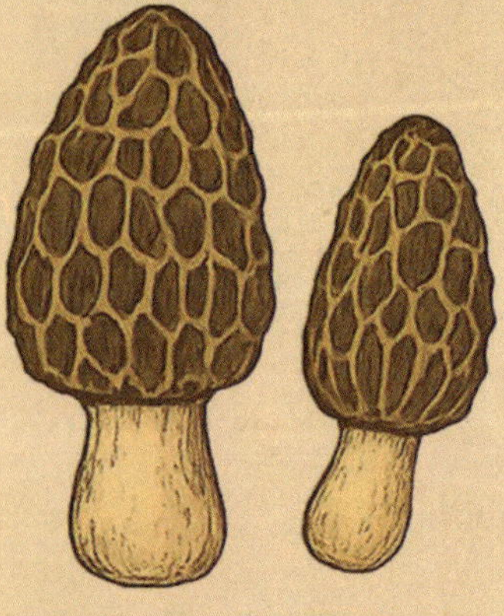

MORELS

(*Morchella spp.*)
Vitamins / Iron

MILKY WHITE

(*Calocybe indica*)
Vitamins B / D

REGIONAL FORAGING INDIA

Termite **MUSHROOMS**
(Termitomyces spp.)
Protein / C Vitamin

Oyster **MUSHROOMS**
(Pleurotus spp.)
Fiber / Protein

Wood Ear
(Auricularia spp.)
Vitamins B / D

PADDY STRAW MUSHROOM
(Volvariella volvacea)
Protein / C Vitamins

REGIONAL FORAGING
CENTRAL/SOUTH AMERICA

COCONUTS
(*Fat*)

CASSAVA
(*Carbs*)

NOPAL CACTUS
(*Vitamin C*)

PAPAYA
(*Fiber*)

Caution:
Stick to known fruiting trees, edible palms, and tribal foraging indicators.

REGIONAL FORAGING
CENTRAL/SOUTH AMERICA

PALM HEARTS
(Calcium, Potassium, Magnesium)

WILD BANANAS
(*Carbs*, Potassium)

AVOCADO
(*High in Fats*)

Amaranth
(vitamin K, calcium, iron, magnesium)

Caution:
Many tropical plants contain alkaloids or cyanides – always boil or roast roots and greens.

REGIONAL FORAGING
CENTRAL / SOUTH AMERICA

Termite
MUSHROOMS
(Termitomyces spp.)
Protein / Potassium Calcium

Oyster
MUSHROOMS
(Pleurotus spp.)
Iron / Fiber / B Vitamins

Wood Ear
(Auricularia spp.)
Iron / Vitamin D / Fiber

Fringed sawgill
Lentinus crinitus
Iron / Fiber / B Vitamins

REGIONAL FORAGING
CENTRAL / SOUTH AMERICA

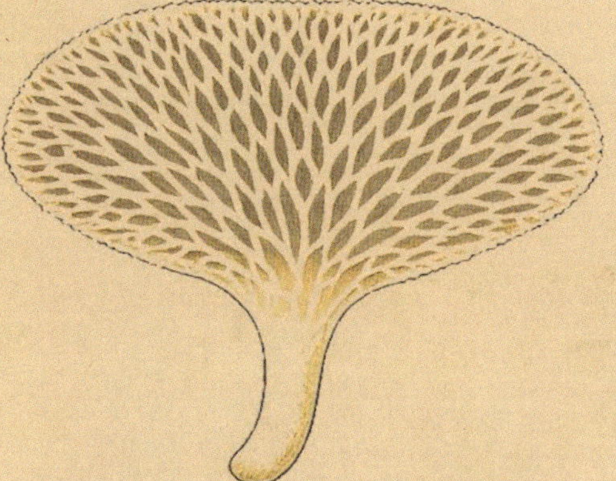

BLACK FOOT POLYPORE
Polyporus tenuiculus
high in carbohydrates

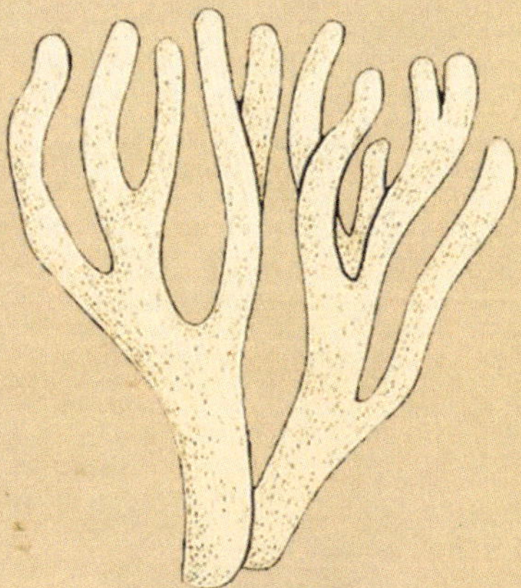

CORAL MUSHROOM
Clavulina spp.
rich in antioxidants

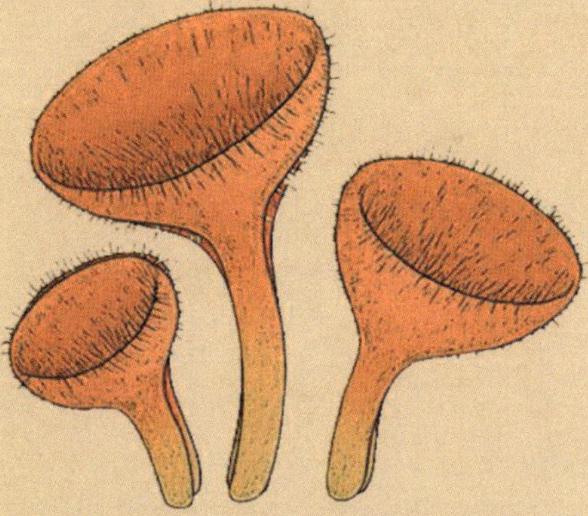

CUP FUNGUS
Cookeina tricholoma
high in fiber

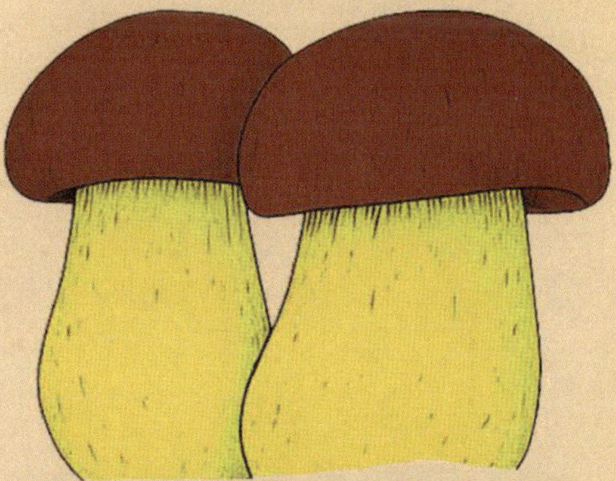

BUTTER FOOT BOLETE
Boletus aureipes
good source of protein

REGIONAL FORAGING
AUSTRALIA / NEW ZEALAND

MACADAMIA NUTS
(*Healthy fats*)

NEW ZEALAND FLAX
(*Sugar*)

FINGER LIMES
(*Vitamin C*)

KANGAROO APPLE
(*Vitamin C*)

Caution: Many wild plants contain toxic compounds or natural defenses that can cause illness if eaten raw. Always verify identification carefully, and cook, boil, or roast roots and greens.

REGIONAL FORAGING
AUSTRALIA / NEW ZEALAND

QUANDONG
(*Vitamin C, Vitamin E, and folate*)

PIKOPIKO FERN
(*Vitamins A,C, and calcium*)

PIGFACE
(*Vitamin C, Calcium*)

BUSH TOMATO
(*Vitamins C, A, E, and B*)

Caution:

Avoid unripe solanaceae fruits (e.g., bush tomatoes, kangaroo apples) – many contain alkaloids.

REGIONAL FORAGING

AUSTRALIA / NEW ZEALAND

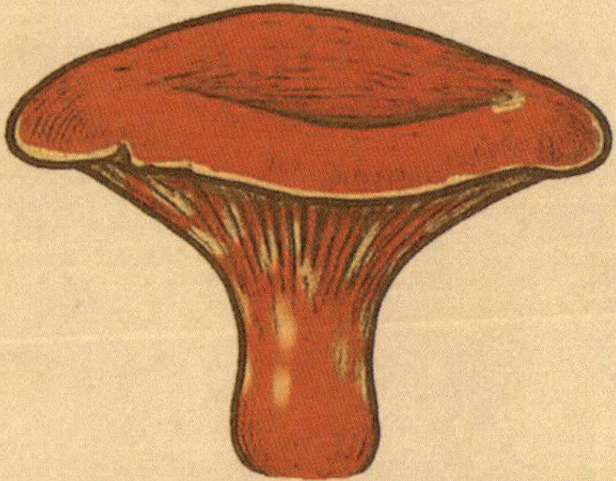

SAFFRON MILKY CAP

(Lactarius deliciosus)

Fiber

SLIPPERY JACK

(Suillus luteus)

Protein/vitamin B

FIELD MUSHROOM

(Agaricus campestris)

Potassium / Zinc

SHAGGY INK CAP

(Coprinus comatus)

Folate / Iron

REGIONAL FORAGING
AUSTRALIA / NEW ZEALAND

WOOD EAR
(Auricularia auricula)

Vitamins B / D

MAITAKE
(Grifala frondosa)

(Hen of the Woods)

Vitamins B / D

PARASOL
(Macrolepiota procera)

Copper / Calcium

WOOD BLEWITT
(Lepista nuda)

Fiber / Potassium

CAN YOU TAKE A USED FLYING SAUCER?
Ghost Works Garage
This baby can fit so many humans!
Ghost Works Garage
GHOST WORKS GARAGE
• LOW MILEAGE • GREAT PRICE •
CALL NOW!
555-1950

CHAPTER 8:

ALIEN SHIPS AND THEIR ENGINES

GREY SPHERICAL CRAFTS

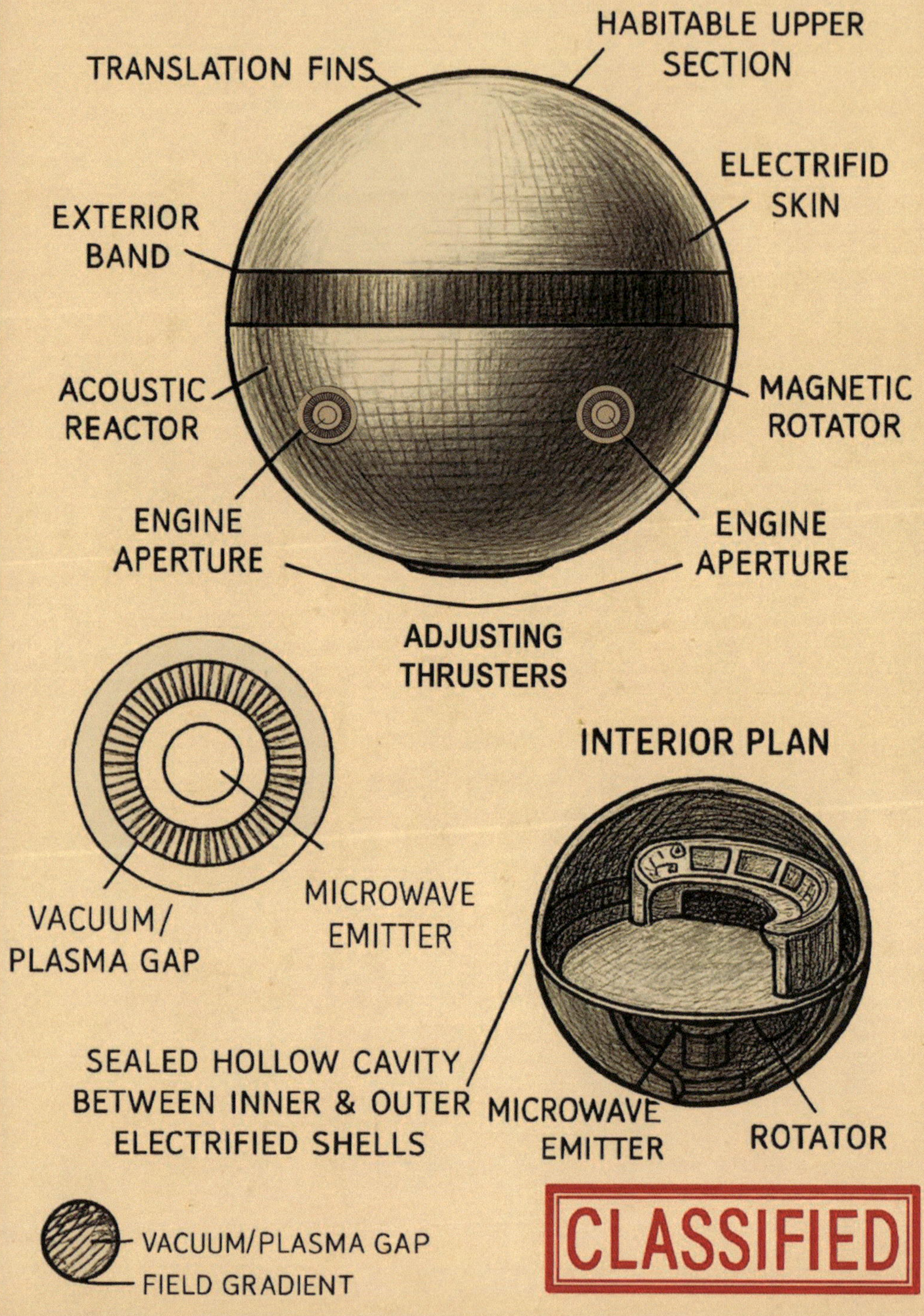

Doc. 24-A
File Log
24597

GREY ALIEN CRAFTS

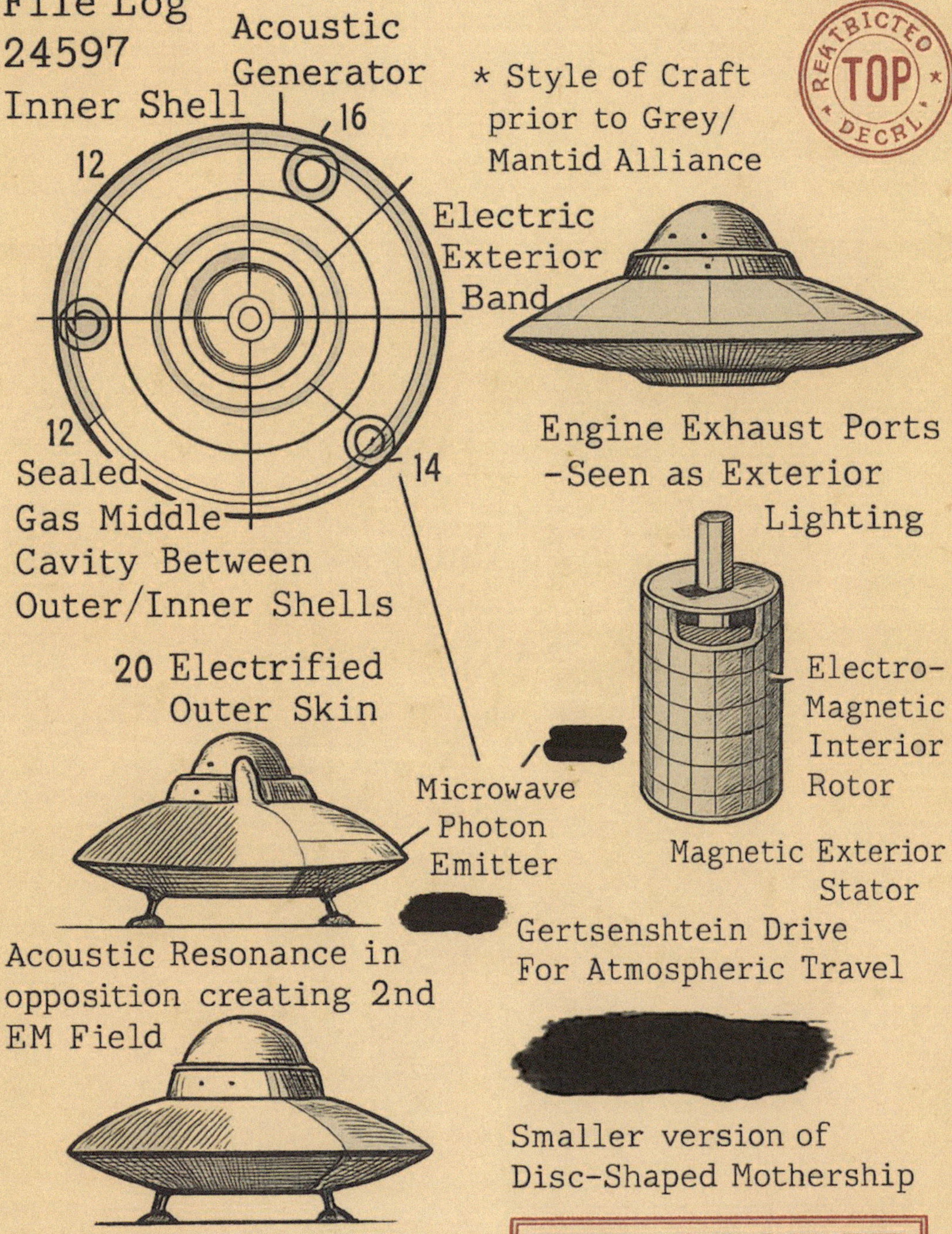

NSA ARCHIVAL No. 819203

TOP SECRET

Peruvian Sample: 23

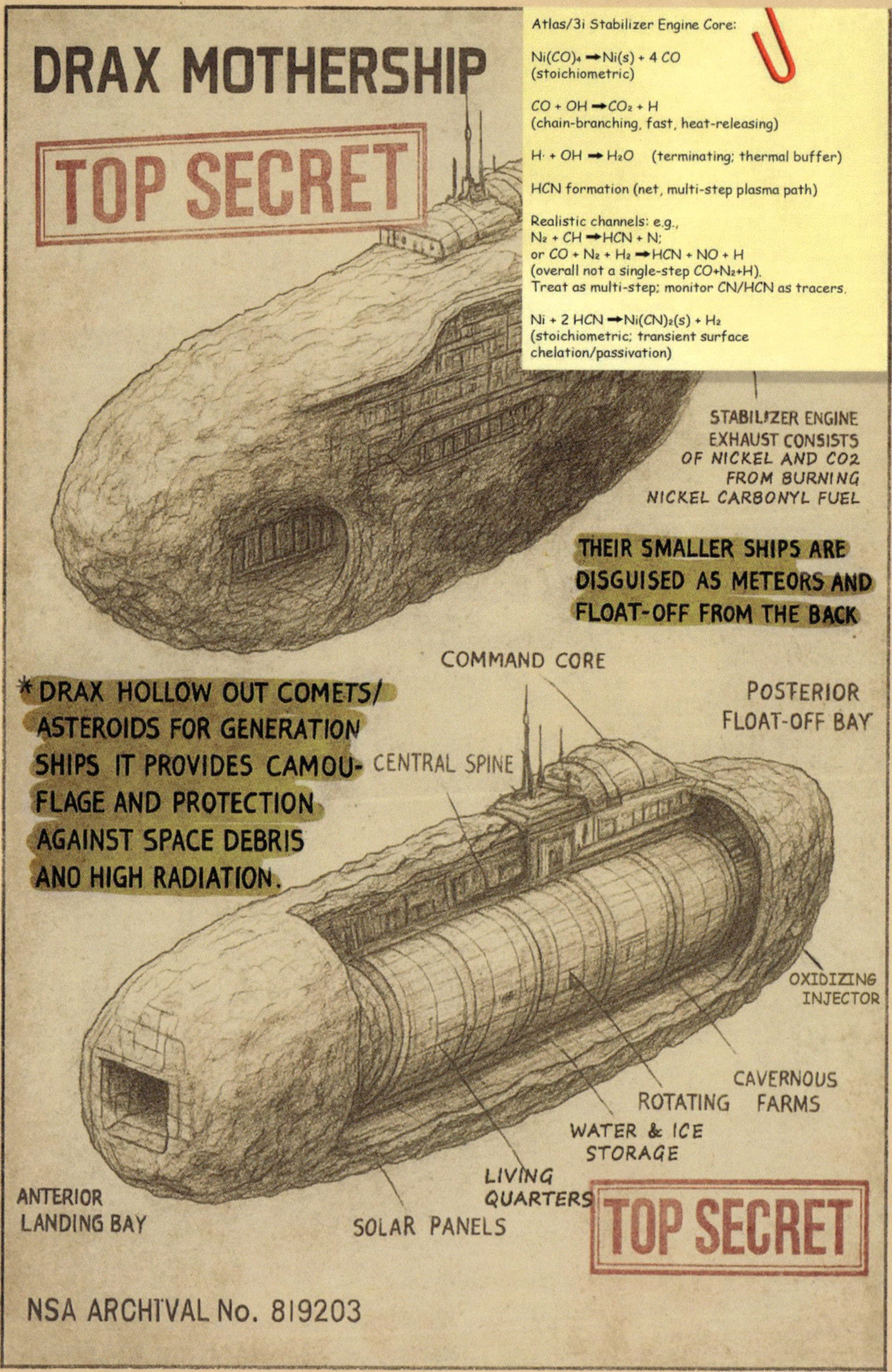
DRAX MOTHERSHIP
TOP SECRET
Atlas/3i Stabilizer Engine Core:
$Ni(CO)_4 \rightarrow Ni(s) + 4\ CO$
(stoichiometric)
$CO + OH \rightarrow CO_2 + H$
(chain-branching, fast, heat-releasing)
$H\cdot + OH \rightarrow H_2O$ (terminating; thermal buffer)
HCN formation (net, multi-step plasma path)
Realistic channels: e.g.,
$N_2 + CH \rightarrow HCN + N$;
or $CO + N_2 + H_2 \rightarrow HCN + NO + H$
(overall not a single-step $CO+N_2+H$).
Treat as multi-step; monitor CN/HCN as tracers.
$Ni + 2\ HCN \rightarrow Ni(CN)_2(s) + H_2$
(stoichiometric; transient surface chelation/passivation)
STABILIZER ENGINE EXHAUST CONSISTS OF NICKEL AND CO2 FROM BURNING NICKEL CARBONYL FUEL
THEIR SMALLER SHIPS ARE DISGUISED AS METEORS AND FLOAT-OFF FROM THE BACK
COMMAND CORE
POSTERIOR FLOAT-OFF BAY
* DRAX HOLLOW OUT COMETS/ ASTEROIDS FOR GENERATION SHIPS IT PROVIDES CAMOU- FLAGE AND PROTECTION AGAINST SPACE DEBRIS ANO HIGH RADIATION.
CENTRAL SPINE
OXIDIZING INJECTOR
CAVERNOUS FARMS
ROTATING
WATER & ICE STORAGE
LIVING QUARTERS
ANTERIOR LANDING BAY
SOLAR PANELS
TOP SECRET
NSA ARCHIVAL No. 819203

DRAX LANDER

TOP SECRET

DECLASSIFIED

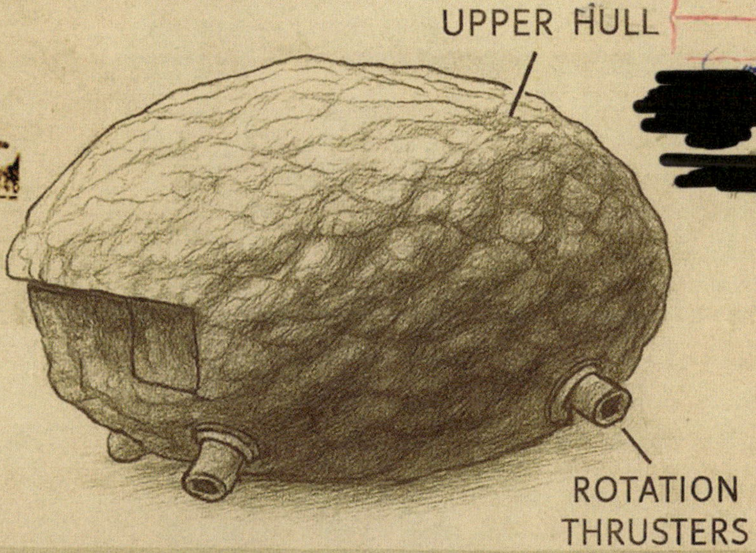

Model used for landing operations on planetary bodies. Resembles a small meteor but with marked thruster scoring.

TOP SECRET

TOP SECRET

NSA ARCHIVAL No. 819203

HUMANOID ALIEN CRAFTS

File Log.
25899

Skull Valley Sample: 213

Technical Field Manual: Extraterrestrial Craft Schematics

SECRET
By Authority of the
Commanding General
Initials Date
OCT

Figure X Space-Fold Engine

- Outer Resonant Torus: phased, high-Q emitter ring Intended to establish nested field gradients.

- Emitter Pods: HF EM/waveguide elements for field shaping and coupling.

- Inner Reactive Cavity: secondary resonant chamber for mode control.

- Central Throat Column: geometry representing the engineered 'bridge' interface.

- Power & Flux Bus: high-density power transmission (fusion/superconducting source theorized).

- Control Array: phase-lock feedback and field stabilization.

Declassified and approved for release by NSA on 06-01-200

- Synthetic 'Fuel' Region: [redacted]

CLASSIFIED

Needs Analysis.
G.H.

HUMANOID ALIEN CRAFTS

File Log.

Fig. X

Skull Valley Sample: 213

~~TOP SECRET~~

Fig. X

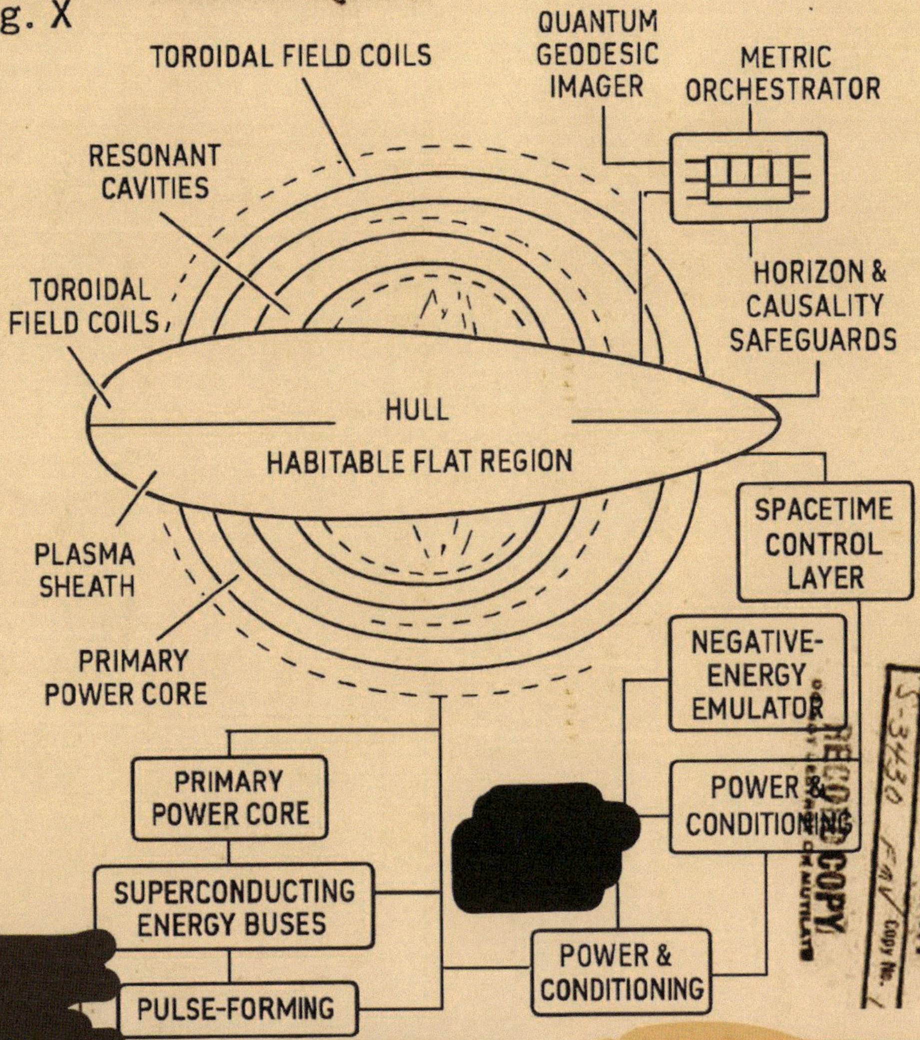

~~CLASSIFIED~~

Designs based off engines
Greys helped them build.
Similar to Alcubierre

MANTID SHIPS

File Log. 25444
Working model
Prototyped

Skunk Wo ollected
near Nuremburg

Dimensional
Harness/
Extractor

TOP SECRET

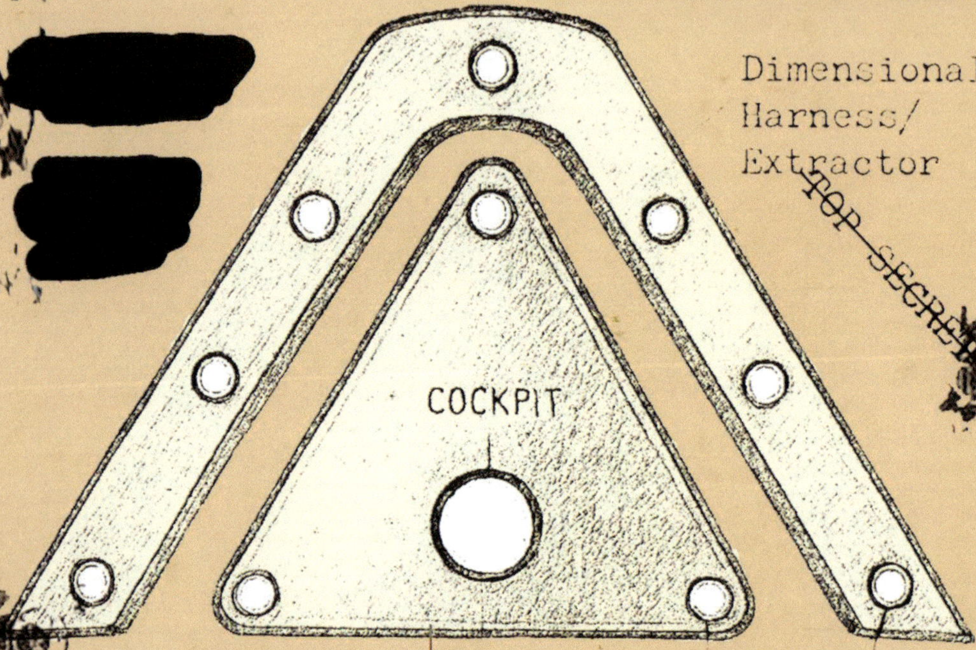

Main Unit

Photon Emitter
Drives

SECRET

SECRET

THE WHITE HOUSE

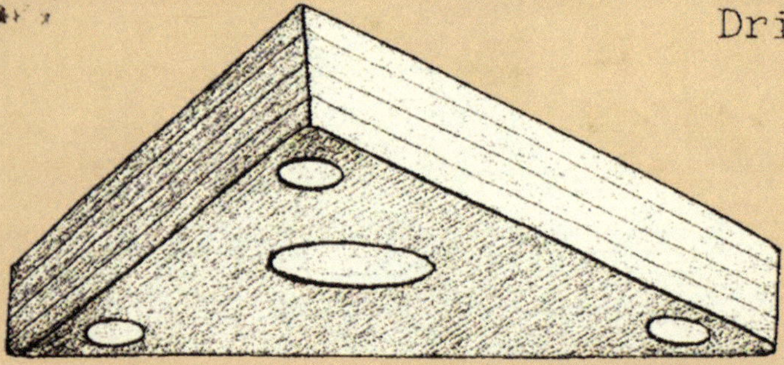

~~No Known Sample~~

MANTIS PERSON

Are they able to cross into our dimension or is it camouflage?

TOP SECRET

TOP SECRET

Shadow People are alien beings but need no ships to come here. Their home is between realities.

TOP SECRET

TOP SECRET

TOP SECRET

SHADOW PEOPLE

Can come through cracks caused by explosions like Nagasaki /Hiroshima

Can be Summoned through Mirrors

TOP SECRET

TOP SECRET
PROJECT BLUE-ISH
BOOK REFERENCE

FURTHER READING: NOTABLE UFO INCIDENTS

Below are 23 of the more extensively studied or debated UFO / unexplained aerial phenomena events, with their locations, informal names, and dates. This list is not definitive, but is intended as a solid starting point for deeper investigation.

#	LUCATION	INCIDENT NAME	DATE / YEAR
1	Nuremberg, Germany	1561 Celestial Phenomenon	14 Apr 1561
2	Basel, Switzerland	1566 Celestial Phenomenon	7 Aug 1566
3	Stralsund, Germany	1665 Celestial Phenomenon	1665
4	Mount Rainier, Washington, USA	Kenneth Arnold Sighting	24 Jun 1947
5	Socorro, New Mexico, USA	Lonnie Zamora Phenomenon	24 Apr 1864
6	Shag Harbour, Canada	Shag Harbour UFO incident	4 Oct 1867
7	Phoenix, Arizona USA	Phoenix Lights	13 Mar 1997
8	Chicago, Illinois USA	Chicago O'Hare UFO	7 Nov 2006
9	Suffolk, England UK	Rendlesham Forest Incident	28 Dec 1980
10	Off San Diego, USA	USS Nimitz / Tic Tac	14 Nov 2004
11	Hudson Valley, New York, USA	Hudson Valley UFO	1982–1986

#	LOCATION	INCIDENT NAME	DATE / YEAR
12	Manitoba, Canada	Falcon Lake Incident	20 May 1967
13	Trans-en-Provence, France	Trans-en-Provence Case	8 Jan 1981
14	Lubbock, Texas, USA	Lubbock Lights	Aug 1951
15	Belgium	Belgian UFO Wave	1989–1990
16	New Jersey, USA	Lights Above the Turnpike	14 Jul 2001
17	Levelland, Texas, USA	Levelland UFO Case	Nov 1957
18	Exeter, New Hampshire, USA	Exeter Incident	3 Sep 1965
19	Berkshire County, Massachusetts, USA	Berkshire UFO	1 Sep 1969
20	Aurora, Texas, USA	Aurora UFO Crash	17 Apr 1897
21	Calvine, Scotland, UK	Calvine UFO Photograph	Aug 1990
22	Gulf Breeze, Florida, USA	Gulf Breeze Six	1987–1988
23	Belgium	Belgian Wave / Phantom	1989

J&J FAMILY PORTRAITS
a unique cosmic portrait experience!
Appointments filling fast!
Call today to make a memory that will last across the galaxy!
VISIT US at 1984 High St.
J&J Photography

LAST WARNING!

IF YOUR NEIGHBORS SHOW SIGNS OF BEING REPLACED, DO NOT APPROACH. CALL THE LOCAL AUTHORITIES.

AGGRESSION MIGHT SPARK AN INTERGALACTIC CONFLICT.

Printed in Dunstable, United Kingdom

72668358R00063